Behind the Walls

Mr + Mrs Kelner,
Best Wishes,
Elizabeth Benjamin

Behind the Walls

Corruption in Our Jails
Cannot Be Ignored for Any Longer

ELIZABETH BENJAMIN

authorHOUSE®

AuthorHouse™ UK
1663 Liberty Drive
Bloomington, IN 47403 USA
www.authorhouse.co.uk
Phone: 0800.197.4150

Published by AuthorHouse 07/28/2015

ISBN: 978-1-5049-8785-1 (sc)
ISBN: 978-1-5049-8786-8 (hc)
ISBN: 978-1-5049-8787-5 (e)

Print information available on the last page.

Contents

Contents

Author's Note

Everything I have written in this book is 100 per cent true. All characters in this book are based on real-life individuals; however, their names have been changed for legal and security reasons. Also for legal and security reasons, and for the purpose of protecting myself and, more important, my family, I do not name the prison that is discussed in this book.

What Inspired Me to Work in a Prison

My childhood and upbringing were fantastic. I, the youngest child of ten, have seven brothers and two sisters. My family always have been very close. My father worked very hard to bring up all of us children. My family didn't have much in the way of money, but we had lots of love and many, many happy times.

Just before I was born, my dad was awaiting the call from the hospital saying that I was delivered. In those days, the expectant father didn't attend the hospital with the expectant mother. Plus, my dad had to be home with all the children. After the call came in and Dad got off the phone, my brothers and sisters formed a line down our hallway. Dad turned to the eldest of my siblings and said, "It's a girl." Those words were repeated all the way down the line – "It's a girl," "It's a girl," "It's a girl" – until the news reached the youngest of my siblings.

Christmastimes were the best. On the cosy nights in winter leading up to the big day, all of us snuggled up together in front of the open coal fire. Our parents did their best in regard to presents for so many of us kids. But the love we all had was everything we needed. Just all of us being together was a gift.

When I was around five years old, things changed in our home because of one of my brothers. My brother Willie is eight years older than me. Before he hit his teenage years, he became, shall we say, a little bit naughty. From the time he was young, he was in and out of trouble with the law. Unfortunately, he ended up being placed in borstals and in young offenders' institutions. Whenever he was in one of those places and away from us, a piece of our family was missing. I remember my mum crying on Christmas Eves and Christmas Days when Willie wasn't with us. At those times, my whole family was distraught.

I remember when I was just a little girl visiting Willie in one of those dismal, bleak places. I could never understand why he couldn't come home with us, why he had to remain there. My parents tried their best to explain to me that he had been naughty and that when he was good again he would be allowed to return home, but this never consoled me. I used to cry for Willie because I missed him very much.

My brother Willie was and is very intelligent. When the time came for him to attend high school, his primary teachers informed my parents that he should apply for grammar school. This he did. He passed all of the exams to get into grammar school. It was a struggle for my parents to fund the schooling, but they did so, thinking that the better school would put Willie on the straight and narrow. He was at the grammar school for just a couple of terms before he was expelled because of his behaviour. He then attended the high school where two of my brothers were in attendance. When Willie was fourteen, he was suspended from high school for his behaviour once again. Not agreeing that he should have been suspended, he said, "If I can't go to that school, then no one can." He then burnt down the school! He received a sentence of three years in a young offenders' home. I cried for what seemed like forever. On the day Willie was sentenced, his solicitor told my parents that he would either turn out to be a solicitor or a barrister, or that he would be the king of the underworld. He never became a solicitor.

When I entered high school, I encountered a lot of grief because of the fact that it was my brother who had burnt down the school. Willie soon put a stop to the taunting I received from other students, after which time I put my head down and simply concentrated on my schoolwork.

During Willie's three-year sentence for arson, he was able to study and take all of the exams that he would have taken had he still been at school. He came out of the young offenders' institution with many A-levels and qualifications. When he was serving that sentence, he absconded once. He took a vicar's bike from outside a church and pedalled around for seventy miles before reaching home. When the police came to our house looking for him, my mum couldn't lie to them. She invited them into our home. But before the police got to the kitchen, which was situated at the rear of our house, Willie had gone out of the bathroom window and had climbed down the drainpipe. He was off on his way again. Eventually, when the police did pick him up and return him to the young offenders' home, he had to serve his full sentence plus a little more for absconding. He had no time deducted from his sentence for good behaviour.

Over the next few years, Willie, up until his early thirties, spent time in and out of different jails. He was around thirty-two years old when he served his last sentence. However, he was innocent of the crime for which he had been convicted. It had been a set-up. Neither his solicitor nor anyone else would take on his appeal, as no one believed he could win his case. So Willie took the case on himself. He took it to the appeal court in London, and he won the appeal. Unfortunately though, our father passed away while Willie was incarcerated (while innocent). Heartbreakingly, Willie was brought to the funeral under prison escort. This was unpleasant for him and unpleasant for my mum and the rest of our family.

Willie never spoke much to me about his times in jail until I was about twenty years old. But I remember something he once wrote to me in one of the many letters he used to send. He told me about when he was younger and had ended up in solitary confinement while serving a sentence. He had been stripped naked and had taken a beating from the prison officers. He said that all he could see was his family at home on Christmas Eve, as that was the night when he was stripped and beaten. He told me many things after that, about how inmates were treated within the prison system and how he himself was treated. At the time of those happenings, he never complained or moaned about what was occurring. Willie could handle himself inside and outside of prison. He was afraid of nothing but the dark.

I began to ponder about Willie's young life in and out of institutions and also about my family's life, what with not having him around as much as we should have.

I had attended court for many of Willie's cases. Some resulted in good outcomes, which meant that he would return home with us. The outcomes of others were not so good. After those hearings or trials, he wouldn't return home with us.

The law intrigued me. Borstals and prisons intrigued me. And Willie's life inspired me. I had gotten the inspiration to see for myself what the justice system was all about.

My Voluntary Work in Children's Homes and My Pursuit of Adult Education

After having my three children and deciding not to have any more children, I was able to concentrate on my career. At that time my husband ran, and still runs, his own business. When he was home in the evenings, I did some voluntary work with the Youth Service. When I first joined the Youth Service, I was shown around four different youth centres by a senior youth worker. All of these youth centres were up and running at the time and were being used by young people. Three of the centres seemed very nice and calm, with the young people playing pool, playing games, chatting, and so forth. Basically, the young people were just chilling out and enjoying themselves. These three centres were all quite close to where I lived, so they would be easy enough for me to travel to.

The fourth centre I toured was on the edge of a very rough council estate. I believe that even the dogs walked around that estate in groups, for their own safety. As soon as the senior youth worker and I entered the building, we saw a group of young people fighting in lumps! I could see the youth workers trying their best to break up the fight, but it looked like a free-for-all. Eventually, the scuffle came to a halt and the situation seemed to calm slightly. At the three centres I had attended previously, the young people had been very polite to me. But in this centre, it seemed like the young people were sizing me up, calling me a stuck-up bitch, and giving me a great deal of hassle.

The senior youth worker and I then returned to the base, where she asked me which one of the centres I would like to work in. She explained that I could go home, have a think about it, and contact her the following day to let her know my decision. I told her I had already made my decision: I wanted to work in the fourth centre where we had been. She looked at me as if I'd gone out of mind before she said, "Why the hell would you want to work in that one?" I told her that I would find it a challenge. I also said that I felt I could make a difference. She just stared at me and said, "Well, good luck with that then."

I worked in the centre on Monday and Thursday evenings. I loved every minute of it. The first few times I attended, I received a lot of verbal abuse from the young people, who all seemed quite poor and very shoddily dressed. The majority of them would just laugh when I tried to make conversation with them. On a few occasions, I and other staff had to call out the police, as the young people organised fights with other groups of young people from the nearby estates. Sometimes these would get out of control. On one occasion, one of the youngsters stole some keys from the team leader and locked us staff in the centre. We were in there for what seemed like hours before someone came to our aid and rescued us.

After a couple of weeks, I decided I would give a pop quiz to the youth. They were all laughing and taking the mickey out of me when I was handing out the quiz sheets. Then I told them that there was a box of chocolates for the one who answered the most questions correctly. That evening was very quiet while the youth were doing the quiz. Bless them, they were all trying very hard to win the chocolates. The activity went down as a treat. They loved it and asked if we could do a quiz every week. So just by giving a simple quiz and offering a box of chocolates to the person who got the most correct answers, I had built up some kind of relationship with the young people.

One evening, I was playing Connect Four with a young lad called Sam. It was going well until I decided to stop letting him win. I won the next game. He called me a cheat and said he was going to get his dad to come up to the centre and beat me senseless. He threw the game across the centre and stormed out, kicking and smashing things as he passed them. I honestly believed that he had gone to get his dad, but he never returned that evening. I was quite sad because it was Sam's last night, as he had reached the age where he was too old to attend the centre anymore. I didn't see him until about five years later, at which time I couldn't believe how much he had changed. The first thing he did when he saw me was give me a hug and apologise for the way he had spoken to me that evening five years prior. He has turned out to be a really nice young man. I see him often now. Each time I do see him, he tells me that I was the best youth worker he encountered.

Later on, there were government cuts. Unfortunately, this meant that the majority of youth centres had to close, mine being one of them. So I then got involved with detached street work, which basically consists of trying to get young people who are hanging around the streets to team up with youth workers to play football and other games. The workers also encourage the young people to join sports centres or community centres. With the cutbacks, this detached street work didn't last very long. Unfortunately, the young people were soon back into the habit of hanging around in the streets, smoking, drinking, and using drugs. It is sad to think that so many clubs and centres had to close, taking away the incentive for many young people to achieve more and to do better.

I then went into adult education. I studied law, psychology, and sociology. This was a brilliant time for me, as I adore studying and learning. I enjoyed the law course the best out of all the courses I took. I studied criminal law, family law, and consumer law. My class used to go on many outings to local courts. I was able to view from the public gallery while taking notes. I learnt so much that it was awesome. I spent hours and hours researching and studying for all of my exams. My husband spent hours and hours helping me and minding the children while I was hard at it. I say that he was my husband, but at that time we weren't married. It was when I was in adult education that we decided to get married – only we didn't tell anyone. We went to Scarborough one weekend and got married. It is said that everyone has a happy place. Well, Scarborough is mine. It's the place where my family spent our holidays when I was a child. That gave me lots of happy memories. Also, I spent a lot of time with my dad in Scarborough before he passed away.

After I finished my college course, I got myself a job as an RSW (residential social worker). I worked with young people between the ages of eleven and eighteen who were living in young people's homes for many different reasons. Some had been abused and some had been in trouble, but the majority had severe damage in their histories. My main role as an RSW was to give the young people in care a realistic chance to recover from their past, to encourage them to believe in their own potential, and to help them build a positive foundation before they reached adult life. We RSWs were there to help the young people emotionally, socially, physically, and educationally, preparing them for independent living in society.

I witnessed many a sad case when I was working with the young people. It can be very hard to comprehend what other individuals have had to endure throughout their lives. The job was a very challenging but rewarding one for me. Sometimes I would be faced with the young people's attempted suicides, absconding, violence, and threats. On one occasion, a girl who had previously been in our care came back to the home to visit another girl with whom she had become friends. It was a night that I will always remember. The girl who came to visit was actually not allowed within a mile of the home, as she had caused a vast amount of trouble prior to her departure (she used to be in care at the home). However, the other girl who was in our care had allowed her to enter the home. When I entered the kitchen and saw them chatting away, I knew that I had to ask the girl to leave. I did this with the utmost politeness, but the girl wasn't having any of it. After several times of my asking her to leave and her blatantly ignoring me, I informed her that I would go get my colleague from the office and that we would have to escort her from the home. As I made my approach to the door, the girl pulled out a knife and put it to my throat. She had me pinned against the kitchen unit. All I could feel was the knife against my neck. Even under those circumstances, I could not let her see that I was scared, although all of my visions at that very time were of my own daughters at home. I thought about what they would do if I weren't there for them anymore. The girl who was still in our care managed to talk the other girl round, telling her that if she hurt me she would go to prison and would not see her friends for a very long time. The girl who was threatening me dropped the knife and ran out of the house. The girl in our care ran to me, put her arms around me, and started to sob uncontrollably.

At the home, the young people threw a lot of anger my way, but overall I found working with them to be special and very rewarding. One girl in particular would not go to sleep at night until I had read her a story. She was sixteen years old. She said she felt comfort from my reading to her before she went to sleep. I also recall a young cockney lad who, whenever I was on shift, wanted me to go fishing with him. I knew nothing about fishing, but I learnt very much from him. He would never speak when he was in the home, but as soon as we got on the riverbank, he would speak for England.

As much as I loved my job, I discovered that I had gone into it at the wrong time. I had three young daughters and a husband at home. My youngest daughter was only two years old at the time. I was contracted for part-time hours; however, because of a shortfall of staff, I was doing full-time hours and, in some weeks, working more than full-time. On the shift patterns where it was on my rota to do a sleepover, then I would start my shift at 2 p.m., work up until 11 p.m., go to bed, start my shift again at 7 a.m., and then finish my shift at 2 p.m. So I was actually away from home and my daughters for over twenty-four hours. Some weeks, what with the shortage of staff, I would do two or three of these sleepovers. I could not work that number of hours and look after my young family at the same time. I decided to give my notice, saying that when my family had grown up, I would return to that type of work.

Being an RSW was the most rewarding job I have ever done. It was also very sad when I left the young people behind. In that type of job, workers are not allowed to have any contact with the young people outside of working hours. This rule applied to anyone who left the job. Unfortunately, I couldn't have any contact with any of the young people with whom I worked. This was sad for me, especially years down the line when I heard that the young girl to whom I used to read ended up in jail and took her own life while in custody.

The Prison Service

After leaving the young people's home, I concentrated on my family. Up until this point, I had managed to have a part-time job so as to fit in with my young girls' and my husband's schedules, but it was always in the back of my mind that I would like to work for the Prison Service. This was the job I wanted, the career I wanted.

In 2006, when my youngest daughter was eight years old, I started with my applications. I had seen that my local prison was recruiting, so I sent off for the application. I went through the application process and thereafter got an interview. I attended the interview. About three to four weeks later, I got a reply saying they were sorry that on that occasion I had been unsuccessful. That didn't stop me. I continued looking, searching, and waiting for recruitment campaigns or any jobs opening up within the Prison Service.

Within a few months, my local prison was recruiting again, as was another local prison. So I applied for both of those jobs. I went through the application process and got interviews at both of the local prisons. When I attended the interview at my local prison, one of the officers on the panel was the same officer who had interviewed me the first time. She remembered me, as she commented on the fact that I was persistent.

I went for the interview at the other local prison the following week and had a feeling that the interview had gone really well. Within a couple of weeks, I received a letter from this local prison saying that I had been successful and offering me a place. I was overwhelmed. However, at that time, once a person had received an offer of employment, he or she was then placed on a waiting list. Straightaway, I accepted the offer. It was just a matter of awaiting my place. The prison staff estimated that it would be around six to eight weeks. During that time, I also received a letter from my local prison saying that I had been successful and offering me a place. I was elated with two interviews and two acceptances. Once again, if I accepted, then I would be placed on this prison's waiting list. I was absolutely delighted. Not only had I gotten the job I had always dreamed of, but also I now had my choice between two prisons.

One of my first experiences of the arrogance of certain prison officers occurred just after I had accepted the post at the second local prison. In my local pub with my husband, I was telling a fellow patron that I had received an offer and had accepted the offer to work at that particular prison. I was aware that this man worked at my local prison, but I only really knew him from seeing him now and then in our local pub. I asked him what would be expected of me and if he would give me some background on the prison. He told me he had just been promoted from prison officer to senior officer. This was obviously a really good promotion on his part. I offered him my congratulations. He then actually gave me some good advice and told me that any time I needed any help or any advice, I should just contact him and he would do all he could. A month or so later, I saw him again. By this time, I had made the decision to work at my local prison. I told this fella that I had been offered the post at the local prison and that I would see him within the prison once I had done my training. He then had to come clean and tell me that he wasn't a senior officer. He hadn't gotten a promotion. He was just a prison officer, as I had presumed. He gave me some cock-and-bull story that he had passed all his training and exams for the promotion but then decided against taking the job. Common sense tells me that no one would do that. Then he said to me, "Don't be offended if I don't speak to you in the prison. It's just that not many prison officers speak to OSGs, cos they stole our jobs. I can't really be seen talking to you."

OSG stands for "operational support grade". That is the role that I applied for at both my local prisons. Basically, it is a step into the Prison Service. With training and time, an OSG can work upwards on the ladder right through prison officer to senior officer to principal officer and so on. OSGs are employed for a wide variety of duties, including checking in visitors, supervising visitors, patrolling perimeter and grounds, supervising work parties, escorting contractors and vehicles, searching prisoners' property, performing store duties, doing routine administrative work, and performing switchboard and control room duties. A lot of prison officers did not agree when the Prison Service instituted the role of OSG. Those officers who were against them referred to OSGs as JSBs, the latter meaning "job-stealing bastards". They looked upon the situation as this: they were stuck on the wings with the prisoners while the OSGs were doing the other duties mentioned above. So this was the reason why the fella from my local pub said that he couldn't be seen talking to me inside the prison. It was pretty sad, really.

After having all the security checks done, I received a date to commence my training. The training was a two-week course at the prison. I believe now that the Prison Service does the training at Newbold Rebel, which is where the training sessions are also held for the prison officer role.

Training

I had done my research on my local prison and was aware of the background and the history of the jail. It was an eighteenth-century jail used as a house of correction. As the population and crime increased in the area, the premises were necessarily enlarged. Additions and alterations to the prison were often being done. A chapel was set up, and a new hospital and cells were added. Given the regular increases of the population of this house of correction, a new, major building was erected in the early 1800s. The major part of the present prison building was erected in the mid 1800s. In 1878, the Prison Service was formed. This house of correction became a prison at that time. Many executions took place at this prison in the early 1900s.

My local prison is one the largest high-security prisons in western Europe. It is also one of the oldest. It is the one of the largest lifer main centres in the country, holding an average of 420 prisoners who are serving life sentences, most of them in the first few years of their sentence. The balance of the prison population are serving 4 years or more.

The prison houses both Category A and Category B prisoners as well as unconvicted Category A's (those held on remand). In addition, this prison houses some of the country's most exceptional-risk prisoners.

I wasn't afraid of entering the prison, but I was apprehensive about the unknown. I'd had my interview in the prison but had only entered the administration department. I knew now that I would be going into the main prison. I was on my own and had no idea how many people would be on the training course, so I was a bit nervous. My husband took me down to the prison and dropped me off after he wished me well. I took a deep breath and entered into the gatehouse. Firstly, before I went anywhere, I had my photo taken for my identification. Then I went through the search procedure. I was told to go wait in a small waiting area and that someone from training would come and get me. There was one other person waiting in the waiting area, a big-built guy who was about fifty years old. He gave me a nice smile and asked if I was there for training. I told him I was. We started a conversation with each other. Not long afterwards, a woman came into the waiting area. She was also there for training. All three of us got on immediately, which was great. We all felt a little more at ease.

We waited about twenty minutes before an officer from the training department came in and introduced himself. He then took us all upstairs to the training rooms. We were told that we were the only three new starters on the training course. Kelvin and I were there for the role of OSG, and Anthea, who was a nurse, was joining the healthcare department. The officer was a Welsh guy, and he was really nice. He told us a bit about what the training involved and then passed us on to the officer who would be doing our first day's induction.

So the training commenced. It was February 2008. I had been given the offer of employment six months prior to this, but it took that long to do all of the security checks and to get my placement with the prison.

The officer doing our induction was very loud. He spoke very fast and spat everywhere while speaking. I could hardly understand him, as he threw a mixture of loudness, rapidness, and saliva about. He told a lot of stories about his own history in the Prison Service and bragged about how he was one of the only ones who had "done" Charlie Bronson. He rabbited on and on about how hard he was and how prisoners had feared him in the past. He was actually a negotiator for the times when there was a hostage situation. However, he had been moved from the wings to the training department, as he had been caught forcing a bacon sandwich down an Asian prisoner's throat!

After the talk of his own background, the officer read out the statement of purpose for the prison. "This prison serves the public by keeping in custody those committed by the courts. Our duty is to look after them with humanity and to help them lead law-abiding and useful lives in custody and after release." I don't believe for one minute that the Asian prisoner was looked after with humanity. The officer then read out the race equality policy statement. "This prison is committed to racial equality. Improper discrimination on the basis of colour, race, nationality, ethnic or national origins, or religion is unacceptable; as is any racially abusive or insulting language on the part of any member of staff, prisoner, or visitor, and neither will be tolerated." Then came the best one, the equal-opportunities statement:

> This prison is opposed to any form of discrimination or harassment; whether direct, or indirect, conscious, or unconscious, on grounds of ethnic origin, religious belief, sex, sexual orientation, disability, or any other irrelevant factor. Insulting, abusive, or derogatory language will not be tolerated. Any form of harassment or discrimination, including sexual and racial harassment, will be regarded as a serious disciplinary offence.

It is my opinion now that not one bit of the statement above stands correct.

The first week of training was basically all about prison security, searches, and authorised and unauthorised items within the prison. After that came radio training, control and restraint, hostage situations, and how the prison runs on a daily basis. On our very first day, Kelvin, Anthea, and I were taken onto the wings. We watched the procedures during mealtimes, lock-up, and association. I was mesmerised! The whole thing just astounded me and took my breath away. The wings, the prisoners, the staff – the whole running of the prison opened my eyes. It was like another world in there. I wanted to stay the whole day and carry on with observing how everything was run, but we had to move on.

We three trainees were then taken to what I thought was the worst part of the jail, the segregation unit, which is better known as the block. This wing accommodates vulnerable prisoners as well as prisoners from the main wings who have done wrong. In addition, the wing has a close-supervision centre that houses some of the country's most exceptional-risk prisoners. I have never experienced anything like it before. I realise that there are some very dangerous criminals who are locked up behind bars, but I do believe that they should be afforded a certain standard of living. In the segregation unit, a decent standard of living does not exist. Prisoners in this area are caged up for over twenty-three hours each day, are tormented, and are denied contact with anyone. In such a situation, there are bound to be repercussions. I don't believe that animals should be treated in this way, let alone human beings.

The officer who was showing Kelvin, Anthea, and me around the segregation unit said he was going to lock us up, each of us alone in one of the unfurnished cells. This was to see how we reacted to the locking of the cell door and being in there alone. Apparently, a lot of trainees in the past have either refused to go in or have had to be let out after literally seconds. I must admit that the experience was far from a nice one. The worst part of it for me was when the cell door was banged shut and I could hear the key turning in the lock. Then there was a deadly silence ... just nothing at all. There was a tiny slit of a window quite high up on the cell wall, so there was hardly any light in the cell. It was dismal and bleak. To this day, I cannot imagine how any human being can spend hour after hour, day after day, in such conditions.

Remember the man from the pub who said that he would ignore me when he saw me in the prison? Well, he actually works in the segregation unit. I take my hat off to him and to anyone who works in there. I think it could send someone quite crazy to be working in those surroundings day after day. I certainly cannot imagine what it must be like for one who lives in those surroundings for months or even years.

The training continued. The first two days were quite an eye-opener. The first week in training, apart from the visits we made to the wings, was mainly spent in the classroom. Prior to my training, my expectations were that the training would be intense and thorough. Given that this was a top-security prison, my belief was that no stone would be left unturned during the training. I also figured that the training would be in depth and would be followed up by tests and maybe an exam. How wrong I was. Most of the knowledge I learnt was from a prison handbook that I read when I returned home on an evening. The trainers left us trainees alone in the classroom a lot of the time and gave us two-hour lunch breaks. Once we returned from lunch, we made coffee and awaited the end of the day, when we would leave the prison. The lack of training we received was pretty unbelievable, really, considering the environment we were to work in.

On my fourth day of training, I and the other trainees were in a classroom studying health and safety. Today we had a different trainer, and the training was more intense than it had been in the past few days. The trainer was in the middle of an important speech to us when the classroom door opened and the lesson was interrupted by a woman officer. She looked over at the three of us who were training and asked, "Which one of you is

Liz?" I raised my hand. She said, "Come with me, please." I followed her out of the classroom. All I could think was that something had happened at home. I began to panic. While I was following the woman officer down the corridor, I asked her if everything was OK, to which she replied, "You tell me." Judging from that statement, I knew there couldn't have been anything wrong at home or else she would have informed me straightaway.

She took me into a boardroom, asked me to sit down, and introduced herself as the principal officer (PO) from the security department. She looked across the table at me and said, "It has been brought to my attention that a member of your family has been in and out of jail and has had trouble with the police. Why have you not disclosed this information to the prison?"

I said to her, "When I applied for the Prison Service and completed the disclosure forms for the criminal background checks, the information required from me was my own details, my husband's details, and my parents' details. There was no request for siblings' details." I also explained to her that my brother had not had a conviction for almost twenty years. She explained that she was going to look into this matter and then get back to me.

As I was leaving the room, she called me back in and said to me, "Don't worry about it too much. You are only an OSG. I will make sure you never walk those landings."

I was quietly gutted by what the principal officer had said to me. If I had been asked in the disclosure to submit information about my siblings, then I would have done so. I would have had to. This brought me to thinking about who had brought the matter to the PO's attention in the first place. In my mind, it had to be one of three people. I knew only three people who worked in the prison: the guy from the pub and two male officers. I had seen both of the latter when I visited the segregation unit. One of the officers was the husband of the girlfriend of one of my brothers. The other officer was a former boyfriend of mine. I believe it was the latter who told the PO about my brothers. He never liked my brother Willie. When I was courting this guy, Willie had a few choice words to say to him. Not long after that, the guy ended the relationship with me. He told me he felt intimidated by my brother and also felt that he would never be good enough for me. So I do believe it could have been him who went to the security department and informed the staff there that my brother was a bad boy.

Upon my return to the classroom, my two new friends Anthea and Kelvin asked me why I had been taken out of the class. I was embarrassed, but I told them the truth. They were both astounded and couldn't believe what the PO had said to me. When I returned home that night, I sat and cried. I thought that I was going to be omitted from training and be told that I had no career in the Prison Service. My husband reassured me that they wouldn't do that. He also reminded me of the law change stipulating that no one person is responsible for his or her sibling's actions.

On the second week of training, we trainees were handed our keys and key chains. We were given a list of all the different departments in the prison and were then informed that we had to visit each department and get the list signed upon our departure from each to prove that we had been there. This was quite an experience, as we had not been trained on matters involving the keys and the gates. Some gates in and around the prison were electronic gates, so no key was needed, obviously. Unaware of this, we tried to unlock some of the gates but couldn't, because they were the electronic ones. Then we would be standing for ages at some gates, waiting for them to open while thinking they were electronic, but they were the keyed gates. Apparently, the control room staff have a good giggle when new staff arrive, as the former can see the latter struggling with the gates. Established staff watch new staff to see how long they will stand at a normal, locking gate while waiting for it to open.

Kelvin, Anthea, and I made our way around the prison, getting our lists signed and trying not to get lost. It was very interesting to see all the different places. Most of the staff we came across were quite accommodating with us and were keen to inform us of things and show us around. However, some of the staff were just pig ignorant. We could tell that they didn't want us there, as they moaned when we told them that we were new starters and asked why it should be them that had to show us round. Some of them commented, "More job-stealing bastards." The reception area staff were not very helpful either. They didn't speak much and just let us wander around aimlessly. Part of the purpose of visiting these departments was so that staff could give us insight into how their department was run, the schedules they had, and the basics of the day-to-day running of the prison.

Three departments that we visited stood out to me. I could have stayed all day, given the chance. The first was the prison library. It was very peaceful and tranquil. I know that libraries are supposed to be peaceful and quiet. This library was full of inmates and very few staff, yet the place remained calm and quiet. There were some inmates doing work on the computers and other inmates reorganising books on shelves. They were all very pleasant, referring to me and Anthea as Miss and referring to Kelvin as Boss. There were a lot of Charlie Bronson's artworks on display in the library, including all the artwork for the charities he was involved in. I thought his artwork was very good. Each piece seemed to tell a story.

The second department I found inspiring was the woodwork shop. This was one of the workshops where inmates attended work during the day. I believe that most of the inmates in there were trusted inmates, given the amount of tools that were within sight and in use. The officer who was in charge was a lovely guy. He spent a lot of time explaining to us new hires how the woodwork shop ran. He showed us around and told us all about the charity work the inmates did in there. It was very relaxed in there despite the fact that there were a lot of inmates around and a lot of woodwork/carpentry tools laid about. Some of the woodwork that the inmates were doing was unique – out of this world, actually. Some were making dolls' houses and furniture for inside the houses. Every piece had been handmade and was crafted to include great detail. I could see just how much work and how much patience had gone in to each piece. Some inmates were making statues or towers or buildings. One inmate was constructing a full mini village. He had completed the houses, shops, and roads and was just starting with a chapel. It was really amazing.

The third department I liked was the Braille workshop. Here, inmates were transforming normal books into Braille books for the blind. There were around fifteen inmates in this room, all sitting at desks and doing their jobs. The work was quite difficult too. I believe that the inmates had to pass a special kind of course to get into this workshop. The jobs here were much sought after. Most of the work the inmates were doing at that time was transforming A-level studying books into Braille books for blind students. I thought this was remarkable. I myself am blind in one eye. I lost my right eye in 1991 because I had a melanoma tumour at the rear of the eye. Even though I still have sight in my left eye, I fear how I would cope if anything went wrong with the one eye remaining. So for me, seeing what the inmates did in the Braille workshop was touching and meant a lot to me.

We visited the healthcare department a couple of times, as Anthea was going to be working within that department. This department certainly was an eye-opener. The healthcare department was meant for the ill and the vulnerable. There were quite a few high-profile inmates in there at that time. The first time the three of us entered, we just used our keys and went inside. No one informed us that if certain inmates were out of their cells, then staff could not enter. There were all kinds of weird inmates walking around the healthcare department, giving us the eye and trying to figure out who we were and what we were doing there. There were a couple of occasions when I could feel someone behind me. I got that tightening-of-the-back-of-the-neck feeling until the person passed. Anthea was very dubious when we first went it. She was going to be working in there all the time. Everyone to whom we spoke around the prison who knew that Anthea was working in healthcare would say to her, "Oh dear. So you're the one who's gonna brave working in there then." She would just look at me and Kelvin and shudder. She had been in nursing almost all her working career, but never in a prison – and never a high-security one at that.

After two weeks of training within the prison, it was time for us trainees to be allocated our jobs. Kelvin and I were aware where Anthea was working, but we were unaware where we ourselves would be placed. I was just hoping and praying that I would be placed with Kelvin. He sort of took me under his wing from day one. He was older than I by about twelve years, I believe. He was a lovely man, one who told it how it was. For Kelvin, a spade was a spade. He was quite a big-built fella too, so no one would particularly want to mess with him. We got on straightaway as soon as we met, as did Anthea and I. We all got on very well together, but I knew that Anthea would be going to a different department. I really wanted to be able to stay with Kelvin.

One of the training officers approached me and Kelvin to tell us that the works department was short-staffed and that we would be allocated there. He explained that it would be Monday to Friday with every weekend off, unless there was any overtime. If there was, then we could work weekends if we wanted to. He also informed us that there was a massive lighting and security upgrade just starting, and also talks of a new kitchen being built. The work would involve escorting contractors and staff around the prison, maintaining security measures at all times, logging work tools and vehicles, and seeing to the health and safety side of having contractors and vehicles within the prison. Kelvin and I would be shadowing other members of the works department staff for two weeks, and then we would then be trained well enough to take on the role ourselves. The training officer did say that if we thought we would experience any difficulty from working outdoors during the winter months, then he would put us on operations duties. Both Kelvin and I were quite happy to go to the works department, especially with the prospect of having weekends off. So we both signed the forms and put on the finishing touches regarding ordering the correct uniforms and work boots, etc. We finished the training on Friday afternoon and were told to report to the works department on the following Monday morning at 7.45 a.m.

Works Department

Monday morning arrived. I was up bright and early, uniform on and all ready to start what I thought was going to be the career I had longed for. My husband and daughter wished me luck, and off I went. I met up with Kelvin in the prison car park, and we went into the prison together. It was the usual routine through the search area: boots off, belts off, all bags through the scanner, and then walk through the body scanner. I bleeped straightaway, which summoned me to have a rub-down. From my first day in the prison to my last day in the prison, I had to have a body rub-down. This was because I have a magnet at the back of my false eye which is stitched to my muscle, so it is a permanent part of me which cannot be removed. I always need to be searched when I go through the airports, as the same thing happens there.

So Kelvin and I headed down to the works department once we had gone through search and collected our keys. We met with the principal officer of the department, Mr H. He was an incredible man, as I came to find out in the next few months. He was one of the nicest fellas I had ever met (apart from my father). Mr H went through a few things with us, then told us to go sit in the porta-cabin outside the works department, where we would meet with the rest of the team, who would show us the ropes. There were twelve of us altogether, including me and Kelvin. A nice set of people, they all seemed to live pretty local. While we were sitting and waiting for everyone to arrive, I noticed that I was the only woman, so I asked one of the blokes if I was the only woman in the group. He told me there was another woman who would be turning up any minute. He said that her husband also worked in our group. Within a few minutes, the couple turned up. The group introduced me and Kelvin to them.

We all then went down to what used to be the boiler house. This was where we would be based within the prison. All of the tools and the vehicle plant were kept there. Also on the premises were a porta-cabin for our team, a porta-cabin for the contractors, and some offices for the bosses. That first week, Kelvin and I shadowed the other staff. It didn't take long for me to get the idea of the job: using the radios and keys, escorting contractors around the prison, doing tool checks, and maintaining the high standard of security required. Within two weeks, we were all good to go. After that, we escorted alone without shadowing other staff members.

Over the next few months, I made friends within our group. It was a really good team. I always thought it a bit strange about the married couple Adam and Eve though. Not only did they work together at the same establishment, in the same department, and on the same shift, but also they always opted to escort together. They were never apart. On Fridays, when Mr H gave us our rotas for the following week, if Adam and Eve weren't marked down as working together, then they would just take it upon themselves to go out escorting together. I don't believe this was a love thing; rather, I believe that each simply didn't like the other working alongside the opposite sex. However, since I was the only other woman in our group, I would be partnered with a bloke if I wasn't escorting with Eve. I didn't see this as a problem at all. Still, for some reason, Adam didn't like Eve working alongside anyone else but him. Likewise, Eve didn't like Adam working alongside anyone else but her. I found this to be a bit of a funny carry-on. Also, before they joined the Prison Service, they worked together at a catalogue company. I love my husband greatly, but I wouldn't want to work with him every day. What would we talk about at night? Putting this aside though, Eve and I became quite good friends. Eve and Adam came to my house on numerous occasions. My husband and I enjoyed a few nights out with them. Their daughter was around the age of our daughter, so the two girls also became friends. My husband set Adam and Eve's son on as an apprentice plumber for a while. So, yes, we became quite good friends.

After a few more weeks, another woman, Kerry, was allocated to our group. Eve didn't like her from day one. A few of the group didn't like Kerry, but I got on fine with her. She stood out, Kerry did, because she wore vast amounts of make-up and had a bit of a funny hairstyle: bleached blonde hair shaved at one side and left long at the other. But she had a reason for the way she styled her hair and for the amount of make-up she wore. A few years previous, she had been involved in a bad car accident. Apparently, she went straight through the windscreen of the vehicle. She lost a bit of her head and was badly scarred. So the vast amount of make-up was to cover the scarring. I believe that parts of her hair were stitched into her head. Because of this, she got a lot of stick and was laughed at.

Kerry was a bit naïve. To start with, she believed everything she was told. A few of the blokes in our group picked up on this and used it for their own amusement. Tamwar, an Asian guy who worked with us, was one of the worst. He was a great guy, but he liked to take the mickey out of people. When Kerry was shadowing with Tamwar one day, he got her to do a tool list with one of the contractors. Almost everything has to be logged down on a tool list for obvious reasons in a high-security prison. The contractor was showing Kerry all of his items when he came to a hammer. She wrote "Hammer X1" on her list before Tamwar asked her if it was a right-handed hammer or a left-handed hammer. She replied, "Oh, I'm not sure. I will ask the contractor." After she asked the contractor, he went into ruptures of laughter. Tamwar then told Kerry to ask the contractors how much petrol or diesel they had in their vehicles, as this would determine how far an inmate would be able to travel around the prison if he managed to break into one of the plant vehicles. Again, she asked the contractors when doing her tool lists how much petrol or diesel they had in their vehicles. She became a laughing stock. I took her to one side and told her not to believe everything she was told.

After a month or so, Kerry became quite unhappy at work. For some reason, Eve would not speak to Kerry at all. She wouldn't even acknowledge Kerry when Kerry spoke to her. I asked Eve why she did this. Her reply was, "I don't like her. Simple." I think the worst thing of all that happened to Kerry was done by the control room staff. When she was doing her training and was sent around the prison in order to find different departments and to get used to using her keys, she found herself standing at the electronic gates for long periods of time before the control room staff would let her through. I found out afterwards that the control room staff were just staring at her over the camera and working out their own theories about why her hair and make-up was like it was. This is why she was always waiting for the gates to be opened. So she passed a comment to the training officer, the one who spat when he spoke, saying that she thought the control room staff should do their jobs properly and stop having her wait at the gates all the time. Being the professional person that he was, the officer went up to the control room that day and told the staff that the new starter had been slagging them off. From that very day, the control room staff had it in for Kerry. This I know is true. On occasions when the works department was short-staffed, we would get control room staff to come and work with us. The majority of them told us that they would make Kerry suffer for what she had said. So thanks to the training officer blabbing about the comment Kerry had made (and probably exaggerating the truth), her life would become a misery within the prison.

On one particular day when Kerry was out with some contractors, she had used her radio to ask the control room to plot the move. Her intended move was simply twenty metres away from where she and the contractors were, but an OSG can't just move contractors around the prison. Permission is required from the control room, just in case there are inmates being moved about. The weather that day was atrocious. It was banging down with rain. It was windy and cold – just a terrible day, weather-wise. The move Kerry had requested was to a place where it would be impossible for any inmates to be, so the move should have been granted. The control room did grant her move, but they told her she had to go via a different route. This route literally entailed walking the full circuit of the prison in order to get back to where she needed to be. There was no valid reason for this move that the control room granted her. The staff did it purely to get back at her. We could all hear on our radios the move Kerry had been given. A lot of our group found it highly amusing what the control room staff had done to her. If she had been granted the correct move, then it would have taken her thirty seconds to move the contractors. Instead, we heard her finish her move in about twenty minutes. When she came back to the compound, she looked like a drowned rat.

Then there was the time when someone from our department planted a glass Nescafé jar in Kerry's bag. I know that a coffee jar doesn't sound like much, but for obvious reasons, glass jars and bottles are unauthorised objects in a prison. The main reason for this prohibition is that staff don't want an inmate getting hold of anything made of glass. Another reason for this is that one inmate managed to push a Nescafé jar up his backside and pull out all of his intestines, which was a bit of a mess for the officers who found him. On one of the mornings when Kerry was coming through search, she did the usual, put her bag through the X-ray machine. There it was, the Nescafé jar. The person manning the X-ray machine asked her why she was carrying a Nescafé jar in her bag. She didn't have a clue where it had come from. After that, she had to go in front of the governor, who issued her a verbal warning. Kerry was extremely upset. When she arrived down at the compound, she was furious. She knew someone had put the jar in her bag on the previous day before she had left the prison, but on the way out of the prison she hadn't been searched, as there are only random searches when staff make their way out. We later found out who had done this prank. It was one of our team, a person who was not very professional and who certainly had no feelings if he purposely put a colleague in the position of receiving a verbal warning for something she hadn't done. Yes, Kerry should have checked her own bag before entering the prison, but I believe the last thing she thought was that one of her own colleagues had set her up.

Kerry took a lot of grief and stick from the staff around the prison. She started to use her annual leave just so she didn't have to come into work. When her leave was all used up, she began to go on sickness leave, as she couldn't face going into the prison. She would telephone me on an evening and would sob her heart out. I had a word with Mr H at the prison and told him that Kerry was very unhappy at work. I never told him that she was getting bullied and picked on; I just told him she was very unhappy. Mr H said he was aware of the matter. Apparently, one of the contractors had spoken to him about Kerry and about the treatment she was receiving from so-called colleagues. So Mr H paid Kerry a visit at her home. A few weeks later, Kerry returned to work. I think she was only back for a week, and then that was it. She left. She was not in a union, so she didn't have any backing. I believe she had been to see the governor, but the governor didn't do anything about her complaints. She told me after she had left the prison that the only reason she didn't take the prison to a tribunal was because she couldn't afford the legal costs.

Just before Kerry left the prison, we got another new starter, Mitch. From the very first day I met him to this very day, he has been my best friend, the best friend anyone could wish for. I knew as soon as I saw him that he was my cup of tea. Over the next few months, he proved me right. He is the most genuine, truthful, honest, trustworthy person you could ever meet. However, my time spent with him when he first joined the prison was short. This was because just before Mitch started, I had applied internally for a different job in a different department. There was nothing wrong with the works department or the people with whom I worked, but the job became very tedious. I felt like I was going nowhere. Hour after hour, I would be standing in the same place with contractors, not moving anywhere, just counting tools and screws and nuts and bolts. And in the winter months, I would be standing outside for hours and hours in the freezing cold. It was a very boring job, but a job that had to be done. I wanted a little bit more. I eventually wanted to become prison officer, but I first wanted a little more experience in other departments of the prison. Also, I wanted more experience around inmates. So when I saw on the prison's intranet a vacancy for a job in reception, I jumped at the chance. For those of you who don't know the workings of a prison, the reception is where the inmates come through when they first arrive at the prison, the first place they see when entering the prison. They also have to go through reception when leaving the prison, whether it's because they are being released or are simply going for a hospital appointment. If an inmate is on trial and attending court, then he will go through reception. All the inmates' correspondence and parcels received from loved ones have to go through reception. Some of this is sent on to inmates, whereas some is kept in reception, depending on the inmate's status. To me, reception seemed to be a very interesting place to work. I was aware that it could be dangerous if there was a kick-off in there, but I suppose anywhere in the prison could be dangerous. So I applied for the post. I got an interview pretty much straightaway. I heard through the grapevine that another OSG had also applied for the role, only he was the son of one of the governors. I thought at the time that I had no chance, not against a governor's son. When I arrived for my interview, the other OSG was there in the waiting area. We exchanged smiles. Before I knew it, I was called in to the interview room. There were two people there conducting the interview, Karen, who was the senior officer in reception, and Kevin, who was the governor of the reception and healthcare departments. They both seemed very nice. They asked me lots of questions, e.g. why I had applied for the post and what I had done in the past. They seemed impressed with the voluntary work that I had done. The interview lasted about thirty minutes. When we were finished, Karen and Kevin told me they had someone else to interview and said that they would be in touch with me in the next few days. When I came out of the interview room, I wished the other OSG good luck before going on my way. I thought my interview had gone well, but it was at the back of my mind that I was up against a governor's son and that I had been working at the prison for only a few months. In a way, I got it into my head that I would get knocked back for the role.

Three days later, once I arrived at work, my boss, Mr H, asked me to come to his office. Once I did so, he informed me that Karen had contacted him to tell him that I had been successful in my interview and that I had been offered the post. Mr H then explained that I had to wait until he got a replacement for me before he would release me from the works department. This was in September of 2008. A week or so later, Karen called me and told me that when I got some spare time to go to the reception, I should ask the officers there to show me around, as they would give me some insight into the role I would be performing. So this I did. I went up to the reception during one lunchtime and introduced myself. Karen was not there. Two officers, Lester and Stef, were present. Stef showed me around the reception area, but I could tell he didn't want to be doing it. He told me to go introduce myself to Lester, who was in the office at the bottom of the corridor. I bobbed my head into the office and saw Lester sitting at a desk and doing some paperwork. I said, "Hello. I am Liz. I will be joining you soon. I am the one that got the job here."

Lester looked up at me and asked, "What do you want me to do about it?" Then he carried on doing his paperwork.

I said, "Karen told me to come and have a look round and introduce myself." He, totally ignoring me, didn't even look up. I repeated myself, but he did not respond. I thought I had better leave. When I was walking back to my department, I thought that maybe Lester was just busy and didn't want to be disturbed, but I still thought he had been pretty ignorant towards me.

A couple of weeks passed and there was still no replacement for me in the works department. I saw Karen one morning when we were going through the search area. She told me that the reception staff and she were having a team-building day at the coast. They thought it would be good if I joined them. She said it was more of a fun day, that we would spend most of the day in the pub, but she thought it would be good for me to get to know the officers outside of the prison. I said I would love to go but I would have to speak to Mr H about booking leave, as the appointed day was during the week. I would be on duty. She said she would speak to Mr H and explain to him that it was team building and would be good for me. Unfortunately, Mr H would not allow me to go, as our department was short-staffed on that particular day.

In October, Karen called me up to the reception and informed me that she was going away for three weeks. She told me that if, in that period of time, there was a replacement for me, then she didn't want me to start in the reception. I should wait until she returned to work. I asked her why she didn't want me to start when she wasn't there. She answered by saying that the officers would bully me in her absence. She said that they were very strong characters who would bully me if I was on my own. I was quite astounded at what she had said, but I thought, "OK, I will take her advice and wait until she returns. She must know what would be best for me." As it happened, by the time Karen returned in early November, there had still been no replacement for me. I was concerned about this because I was aware that another OSG was needed in the reception area quite quickly and I didn't want them getting someone else for the role. I went to see Karen and explained my concerns to her. She was quite annoyed herself that there was still no replacement for me. She contacted Mr H and, I believe, had a bit of a kick-off with him. It wasn't his fault by any means; it was just circumstantial.

A couple of days later, Mr H called me to his office and said that they had gotten a replacement for me and he would release me the following week. He had informed Karen. She called me up to the reception. When I got there, she took me straight out of the way of the officers and told me that I was on the rota to start the following Monday. However, on that particular Monday, she was scheduled to do a week of nights up on the wings. After that, she would be on a one-week rest. She told me that she didn't cherish the thought of my starting there when she wasn't there, but seeing as I had been long in awaiting a replacement, she had no choice. She said she would leave me a work plan from which to work and that she would tell the officers that they would have to guide me through certain things and help me to settle in. She then said, "If Lester gives you any grief, then tell him to fuck off."

I asked Karen why Lester would want to give me grief. She replied, "He can be very nasty and hurtful. He will demand that you make the drinks for him and the officers cos you are the female. And he will try to put you down. When he starts, take my advice: tell him to fuck off and walk away from him." She told me she would ring me through my first week to make sure I was OK.

For the remainder of that week, I received good-luck cards from my colleagues in the works department. On my last day, we all took snacks into the prison and, at lunchtime, had a bit of a farewell party. It was lovely. I was looking forward to my new job, but I was apprehensive about what Karen had said to me. I said goodbye to my work colleagues on a Friday evening and had the weekend off before my new start on the following Monday.

Reception

Monday morning arrived. I did my usual routine, going through the search area and then into the prison. I made my way to the reception and took a deep breath before I went in. When I walked into the office, where I could hear the staff were congregated, I noticed there were three officers in there: Stef, whom I had met previously when I went to look round the reception; Tom, whom I had not met before; and Adam. I had seen Adam around the prison. An officer whom one would always remember, Adam stood out from any other officer. He had a bald head, was covered in tattoos and piercings, and wore his trousers very short above his Dr Martens boots. He looked more like a convict than an officer. He was very scary-looking and was the type of bloke whom you wouldn't want to bump into in a dark alley. However, when I said good morning to the staff, Adam was the only one who acknowledged me. He told me where to put my bag and coat before he offered me a cup of coffee. He then gave me the work plan that Karen had left for me and told me that if I needed any help, then I should ask him. It reminded me of the saying "Don't judge a book by its cover". The other two officers did not acknowledge me at all. I began to look through the work plan and noticed that Karen had written on the bottom that I should wait for the other OSG to come in, as he would show me most of what was on my work plan. Luckily, after I was there for half an hour, the other OSG arrived and began to show me what I needed to do. My main duties were checking the prisoners' property in the prop room, dealing with mail that came through for the prisoners and the items that they had ordered, making sure prisoner-issue clothing was all in order, and performing numerous duties in and around the reception area. Once the OSG had shown me the ropes, I got on with what I had to do.

It was approaching lunchtime. I wasn't sure what time I was to go for lunch, so I asked Stef at midday if it was OK for me to go to lunch. He looked at me and said, "Do what you fucking want."

I said to him, "Well, I am not sure what time I should go on my lunch."

He repeated himself: "Do what you fucking want." So I went for lunch. My first day in reception, I can say, was not the most inviting or welcoming, but I was able to cope.

Over the next few days, I just went in to work and did what I had to do. The officers weren't helpful at all apart from Adam, who did help me when I was stuck. Near the end of the week, Lester and another officer, Dan, came on shift. Lester was the most rude, ignorant bloke I had ever met. On one occasion, we were all in the main reception area when Lester had gone into the kitchen to make some drinks. When he came out, he was holding a tray with all the drinks on it. He handed the drinks out one by one to the officers. Then he looked at me and asked, "What are you looking at?" I didn't answer him, so he said, "Oh, did you want a drink?"

I replied, "Yes, please. But it's OK. I will go make my own."

He then said, "Damn right, you will. Don't expect me to make you one. You are the woman here, and it should be you making the drinks. So don't look at me like I have done something fucking wrong." None of the other staff said anything to him. I remembered what Karen had told me to do if Lester started, but it is not in me to use bad language or be rude, so I just walked away from the situation.

The worst staff in reception were Lester, Stef, and Dan. They seemed to behave worse when they were together, as if they had something to prove to one another. They made it perfectly clear that I shouldn't be working in the reception area because I was a woman. They said it should be male officers only. Lester went even further by saying that not only should women not be working in the reception, but also they shouldn't be allowed to work in a prison full stop. He was like a dinosaur, as he could not change with the times. It was his belief that women should be at home bringing up the kids and doing the housework. He did not keep his opinions to himself though. He was blatantly sexist and did not care in front of whom he said offensive things. Stef and Dan, who were milder male-chauvinists, were just ignorant towards me. On occasions, they would iron clothes for the prisoners who were due for a court appearance. I don't believe officers were permitted to do prisoners' ironing, but a lot of things that went on at reception weren't permitted.

Stef and Dan would both comment to me that it should be me who did the ironing, as I was female and as ironing was a woman's job. When they wanted to speak to me, which was very rare, they would ask me to come to work in a skirt instead of trousers and to wear stockings and a suspender belt so I could give them a look when there was nothing going on in reception. I never rose to their sexist comments. I would just walk away from them. I began to realise that when Stef and Dan did speak to me, it was only to either slag me off because I was female or ask me to wear provocative clothing in order to give them a kick.

I went out to lunch one day. On my return, Stef said to me, "You are fucking late."

I looked at my watch and saw that I was actually five minutes early. I said, "No, I am not. I am early, if anything."

He came right close to my face and said, "I said you are fucking late."

Adam was in the office when Stef said this to me. He turned to Stef and said, "Leave her the fuck alone. All you do is get at her. Just give her a break." Adam was the only one out of all the reception staff for whom I had respect. He was the scariest bloke I had ever come across, but he was kind to me. Also, he was the only one who stuck up for me and helped me when I asked for help. Many a time, I asked Stef, Dan, Tom, and Lester for help or else asked them how I was supposed to do something and they would turn their backs on me and ignore me.

During my second week in reception, I was working in and out of the property room, doing checks on prisoner property and logging items in and out of property boxes. At this stage, I did not have a key for the prop room, as I was awaiting one to be issued to me. But throughout the day, the prop room was unlocked. It was locked at the end of shift by the last one out. At the very end of the prop room was an area where all the property of prisoners who had died in custody was kept. It was kept there for a length of time in case the families of the deceased claimed it. On one particular morning, Stef asked me if I would go do a check on the dead man's property (that's how he and the other men who worked in reception referred to it). I said I would. I was quite surprised that Stef had actually asked me to do something instead of having a go at me. I walked through all the aisles of property until I reached the bottom where the dead man's property was kept. I had been down there for only about thirty seconds when all of the lights went out. I heard the door bang shut and then get locked. Dan, Stef, and Tom had locked me in. They knew I didn't have a key, and they knew I was right at the very bottom of the room. There were no windows in there, and it was pitch-black. I could not see my hand in front of me. I believe that Dan, Stef, and Tom thought I would be afraid when I was down in the dead man's property area, but things like that don't frighten me. I am not afraid of the dark or of ghosts and spirits and such things like that, but they didn't know that. I made my way back up towards the door, which was difficult for me, not just because it was dark, but also because I have only one eye. I lost my right eye in 1992. As mentioned previously, I had a melanoma tumour and had to have my eye removed in order to save my life. At the best of times, I struggle to see what's on my right-hand side, but I struggle more in the pitch-black. I was locked in the prop room for about twenty five minutes before one of my three co-workers unlocked the door. When I went out, I saw that all three of them were laughing at me. I walked past them before turning round to face them and asking, "Anyone want a brew?" None of them answered me. I wasn't annoyed by what they had done to me, but what if they had done it to someone who was afraid of the dark?

The following week, Karen returned to reception after her rest week. She had not contacted me during my first two weeks like she said she would. She asked me on her return how I had been. I said I had been OK. She asked how the lads had been with me. I told her the comments they had made to me and about the incident in the prop room. She said, "Well, I told you what they were like." And that was the end of that conversation. When Karen had interviewed me, she seemed really nice, but when she returned to reception, she seemed like a different person. She was not a bully, but she simply didn't speak to me when the other staff were there. It really felt like I was not wanted in reception. It seemed that I was not welcome, that I shouldn't be there. All the staff except for Adam made me feel that way. But I loved the job. It was interesting and was very different from the works department. All I wanted to do was to better myself. What chance was I going to have of doing this though, when I was working with staff whom I'd expect would aid and encourage me to get further in the Prison Service but who didn't give me the time of day?

My first late duty was approaching. A late duty is when OSGs go up to the wings with the prisoners' mail, any items the prisoners may have ordered, or items that had been sent in for the prisoners by their families. I looked on the rota to see whom I was working late with. It was Lester, my worst nightmare. I was dreading my shift with him. Unbelievably though, he was great with me that night. He couldn't do enough to help me. When we were walking up to the wings, he told me which prisoners to watch and which he thought would be OK with me. He told me that he would watch my back for the entire time we were on the wings. He also said that I didn't have to fear any prisoners kicking off if they didn't get all they were expecting from their mail, because he would deal with it. And this he did. Lester introduced me to the prisoners, telling them that they would be seeing more of me in the future and that they shouldn't give me any grief. He showed me how everything was processed when handing out items to prisoners, including all the paperwork that was required during the process.

When Lester and I finished on the wings, we began heading back to reception. While we were walking back, he looked at me and said, "Don't worry about me, darling. My bark is worse than my bite." I just smiled at him as we carried on back to reception. Once we were there, Lester said I had done well up on the wings. And guess what? He made me a brew! After our coffee, he showed me how to log all the mail and how to log valuables. I still had about fifty minutes of my shift left when Lester said, "Look, there's nothing to do now. I may as well lock up reception. You may as well go home now."

I replied by saying, "Thank you, and thanks for tonight." He smiled at me and then gestured to the door for me to leave. On my way home that night, I felt like a different person. I thought that this was the start of the staff's being nice to me.

The following morning, I went into work as normal. Lester, Karen, Dan, Stef, and I were congregated in the office. Lester looked over at me and said, "Oh, by the way, I have been in touch with the detail department and told them you owe them two hours' overtime because you took it upon yourself to go home early last night." Karen looked straight at me and asked why I had gone home two hours early. I told her exactly what had happened the previous night, saying that Lester had said I could go early, which, by the way, was forty-five minutes early, not two hours early. Lester turned round and said, "It is not my place, Karen, to let her go early. I am not her superior. You are." He totally denied what had happened. Lo and behold, later that day I got a call from detail saying I had two hours' unpaid overtime to do.

It was the week before Christmas 2008. My former work colleagues from the works department had arranged a night out as a Christmas get-together and had invited me to join them. The night was a Tuesday. Earlier in the day while I was still at work, I mentioned the get-together to Adam. Adam was the only one of my co-workers who spoke to me with any decency. Lester and Dan were in reception at the time and overheard my conversation. Lester shouted very loudly, "Oh, she's going out with the fucking Muppets from the works department. That will be a good night." I totally ignored the fact that he had even spoken.

I went and met my colleagues that night. It was great to be with people who were nice and friendly towards me, and not having digs at me. They asked me how it was going in reception and if I was enjoying it. I told them little bits about how the majority of the officers had behaved towards me and about the incident in the prop room. They were not very impressed by what I was saying. One or two of them advised me to report the other officers. But, like a few of the others said, if you report one officer for wrongdoing or for anything at all, then all of the officers will turn against you. Not only will they turn against you, but also they will stick together, lie, deny, and make the reporter out to be the bad one.

Anyway, my former co-workers and I began to have a really good night. It was like a breath of fresh air to be with my friends. Then, unbelievably, two blokes staggered through the pub door, not blind drunk but well on their way. Lo and behold, it was the PO from reception and the governor from reception, the governor being the one who interviewed me for the job in reception. I don't know how long they had been out drinking, but I do know that Darren, the PO, was a lot worse for wear than Governor Kevin was. They both approached our table. Straightaway, Darren asked me why I was out drinking with the tossers from the works department. I told him they were my friends, not tossers. He became very loud and started having a go at some of my friends, calling them arseholes and telling them they would accomplish nothing in the Prison Service. A couple of the lads reared up to Darren. There followed a fracas between them, especially when Darren tried it on with Adam's wife, Eve! Expectedly, Adam flew off the handle. A few of the lads got between him and Darren. In all fairness to Adam, he would have completely levelled Darren, purely because of the state Darren was in. Then Governor Kevin approached me and asked how I was doing in reception. I told him it was OK. I didn't want to go into any details, as I didn't really think it the time or the place. Plus, not knowing him very well and noticing the fact that he was quite drunk, I didn't know what reaction I would get. But he asked me again and added, "Be honest with me, Liz. I know what they are like in there, and I know they are getting at you." So I was honest with him and told him what the staff had been like with me and how they had been treating me. His reply to me was, "Take your shit or walk away." So that was his advice to me – very classy.

At the end of that week, the officers in reception were arranging to go to the pub opposite the prison for a Christmas drink. They had planned to do it on the Friday after work and just spend an hour or two as a bit of a get-together. I was never involved in these conversations or in the plans the officers were arranging. On Friday, my co-workers and I were all leaving reception at the same time. I was walking out behind the officers. Lester turned round and said to me, "Where are you going? Don't think for one minute you are coming with us. This is men only, no women." I just smirked at him and walked past him. He shouted after me and repeated himself.

Then Stef said to me, "Yeah, he's right. It may be a drink for reception staff, but not for women, just the boys." I left the prison and was quietly upset, as a little piece of me had hoped they would ask me to join them. I wanted them to accept me and get on with me. I thought that with its being the season of goodwill, they just may have made an exception and invited me along. I began to realise that they weren't going to accept me, but I couldn't give up. I enjoyed the job I was doing, as I found it very interesting. I wanted to stay where I was. I went home that night and told my husband what had happened. He couldn't believe that the officers were so sexist towards me and mean to me. He said they needed to get in the real world and stop living in the age of the dinosaur.

I spent that weekend at home, just mulling over the recent events at work. I was disappointed by the fact that I had not been accepted by my colleagues. I was also disappointed by the sexist attitude I experienced from the officers in reception. When I returned to work on the following Monday, I dreaded going inside. Inside my car in the prison's car park, I sat and took deep breaths before I motivated myself to go in. I was hoping that the week would go quickly, as I had some leave coming up over the Christmas period. The officers in reception had a pop at me over that. While I was still working in the works department, my co-workers and I had all booked our leave for the Christmas break. The contractors working inside the prison took a week off over Christmas, so we OSGs were not needed. We could use our annual leave over that period. That part of working in the works department was very good. Not everyone in the department did book leave over Christmas. Those who chose to work were given duties to do elsewhere in the prison. My leave was booked quite a while before I started in reception. When the officers in my new department found out that I had just over a week off at Christmas, they fumed and gave me much grief, telling me I should do the decent thing and retract my leave. Yeah, right.

On that Monday morning, I went into the prison and walked through to reception. I didn't know whom I was on shift with. I was the first one in, so I checked the rota. That morning, it was just me and Lester. What could be better? I was already disheartened at the thought of a new week in reception with the dinosaurs, but now I had to do my first shift with Lester. He came in not long after I arrived. I said good morning to him. He blanked me. I made myself a drink and asked Lester if he wanted one. He blanked me. I would not have lowered myself to his standards by not asking him if he wanted a drink. I asked him and he blanked me: fine. I got on with some property checks and some mail to be sent up to the wings. I would say it was around mid morning when I heard two officers from the wings bring an inmate in. They put him in the holding cells and then had a word with Lester before they were on their way. The inmate was shouting very loud, trying his best to gain someone's attention. When I walked past the holding cell, he was shouting, "Miss, miss, I need to speak to you or speak to someone."

I went into the office where Lester was sitting. I told him the inmate wanted to speak to someone. Lester's first words were, "Fucking nuisance." I didn't know if he was referring to me or to the inmate, ha, but he stood up and went out towards the holding cell. The inmate seemed to me to be in his early twenties. I heard the entire conversation between the two men. Basically, the inmate was supposed to be in court in Manchester that morning. The security van was on its way from outside to pick him up and take him over for his court appearance. However, he had received a message from his legal team that very morning saying that his court appearance had been cancelled and that they would let him know when it was rearranged. He was explaining to Lester that there was no need for him to go to Manchester. He asked Lester if he would cancel the security van. Lester didn't believe him initially, so he contacted the wing where the inmate had come from. Someone from that wing confirmed to Lester that the inmate's report was correct. I still don't know why the inmate would have been taken to reception when his court date had been cancelled.

The inmate was very distressed over the matter. Judging from the conversation he had with Lester, I discerned that he had previously been in the same situation. He had been taken by the security van over to Manchester, only to find that his court appearance had been cancelled. Instead of bringing the inmate back to the prison, the security van took him to Strangeways. By all accounts, he had taken a beating there. That is why he was pleading with Lester to have the van cancelled. Lester told the lad he would get a message through to the drivers and cancel the escort.

Lester came into the office where I was. He phoned up the company. They told him that the van was on its way but that they could radio through to the van and instruct the driver to cancel. I heard Lester say, "Don't worry about it. Don't bother radioing through to cancel. Let the van come." He put down the phone and went out to the holding cell, where he told the lad that the van was on its way and couldn't be cancelled. The lad, close to tears, was shaking and almost hyperventilating.

When Lester came back in the office, I asked him, "Did they not say that they could cancel?"

He looked over at me and said, "Yes, they could have cancelled. They could have radioed through and instructed the driver to go back to base."

Bewildered, I looked at him and asked, "Then why did you tell them not to bother cancelling?"

He replied, "What's it to do with you? Let the little twat go and face getting a good hiding again. It's all he deserves. Fuck him." I was really unhappy with what he had done. To me, it was blatant that Lester wanted the inmate to suffer. I told Lester that he couldn't do that, that it was unfair and he was causing an unnecessary bad situation. He told me to shut my mouth. I didn't want to go out of the office then because I knew the lad would probably start pleading with me. There was nothing I could have done.

The escort came for the inmate. Lester had one great big smirk on his face as the workers cuffed the lad and took him out of the prison.

I would like to make it clear that there are a hell of a lot of evil men within the walls of the prison I worked in. Those inmates deserve to be there. And I don't doubt for one second that the families of victims want these men to rot in the prison. I fully understand that. However, when one works within the prison, it is not his or her job to be judge or jury. That job has already been done. There are rules that have to be adhered to. But there are things that I saw happen between staff members and inmates that were far outside any rule book. Given my experience of working in that prison, I now believe that a percentage of the evil men within the prison's walls are actually staff members.

The incident with Lester and the inmate who went to Manchester was one of a few evil things I saw that week. And like I said, it was the week leading up to Christmas. That very afternoon after the lad had been taken to Manchester, I was working in the property room. I had gotten some big, heavy boxes ready to be posted out of the prison. There was a shelf in the property room that held items that inmates had made and could hand out during visiting times. One item that had been placed there was a replica of the Eiffel Tower. Made from matchsticks, it stood about two feet high. It was beautiful. Perfect. Quite a masterpiece, actually – and it had taken the inmate months and months to finish it. The plan was that his mother was to come to visit him from London just before Christmas, at which time he would hand the replica to her as a Christmas gift. Apparently, the inmate's mum was in her seventies. She had to walk with the aid of two walking sticks and had to get two buses and two trains each time she visited the prison. But out of love for her son, she made this hike each time she visited.

I was preparing boxes to be sent out, as I mentioned. I didn't realise how heavy one particular box was before I lifted it. I almost dropped it. I spun around and, knowing there was a shelf there, let the box drop. I heard a massive crunching noise. I pulled the box away to find that I had dropped the box right on top of the Eiffel Tower! It was a complete mess. It was all smashed in and dented. Oh God, what a mess. I tried very hard to push out the dents, but the more I tried, the worse it got. Mortified, I didn't know what to do. I went back into the main reception area and saw that Stef and Dan had come on shift. Lester had gone, thank goodness. I must have gone pale, because Dan said to me, "What's up with you? Seen a ghost or summat?"

I said, "I really need your help in the prop room. Can you please come with me?" Funnily enough, Stef and Dan both followed me. I showed them what I had done. They cracked up laughing. I explained what had happened and how I had tried fixing the tower, adding that all I'd done was to make it worse. I asked them what I should do.

Stef turned to me and said, "Fuck all ya can do. Just leave it." I told him and Dan that I knew the story behind the Eiffel Tower, about how long it had taken the inmate to make it and also about his mum. I said that I really needed to try to put it right. They both laughed. Stef said, "Fuck it. We will just take it out to him before visiting and tell him that some fucked-up bird in reception kicked the shit out of it." It was a visiting weekend coming up. I wouldn't be there, as I would be on annual leave. I asked Dan and Stef if they would take me up to the wing where the inmate was so I could explain what had happened and try put things right somehow, but all they kept saying to me was, "Fuck it. Don't worry about it. We wouldn't." The only thing they told me not to worry about throughout the duration of my time in reception was the one thing I had done that would upset an inmate.

I finished my shift, went out of the prison, got in my car, and cried all the way home. I was sad not only because of the fact that the inmate had spent months and months making the Eiffel Tower, but also because of the thought of his seventy-odd-year-old mum with her walking sticks travelling all that way and ending up with an Eiffel Tower that looked like it had just been bombed. My husband told me that night that I couldn't right all wrongs. Still, it was I who had done something wrong that day, and my so-called colleagues would not help me put it right. I still don't know what happened during that inmate's visit or if he handed the Eiffel Tower to his mum.

The very next day when I went in to work, I was to witness more wrongdoing from the staff in reception. It was the afternoon and I was doing a late shift, so I believe it was around 1 p.m. when I got into reception. The post had arrived. As one can imagine, there were lots of Christmas cards and small gifts coming into the prison. I started on the mail that had been brought down from the censors. The mailing protocol was that each inmate was given a code for the different crimes he committed. Obviously, paedophiles could not receive letters from children or photographs of children, for example. One of the inmates whose crimes did not consist of paedophilia had been sent a small box of rose-shaped chocolates from a family member. He was allowed this item, so I got it ready to be sent up to him on prop night. I had bobbed out of the office to go to the toilet. On my return, I saw that the officers, Dan, Stef, and even Karen, were eating the chocolates. Karen asked me if I wanted a chocolate. She had tipped them out of the box and onto a plate. I asked her where they were from. She replied they were the ones I had just processed for the inmate. I said, "Well, aren't they meant for him and not us?" Dan and Stef started laughing at me, calling me "Little Miss Prim and Proper" and telling me that they had altered my logging of the parcel received and that the inmate would never know. I told them I thought it was wrong what they had done and that, no, I didn't want a chocolate. They all sat and stuffed their faces with the chocolates. I know it was only a box of chocolates, but was it right what they did? Funnily enough, this very same inmate had quite a few items and letters sent in to him that he never received. I cannot name him for legal reasons, but I think he was disliked by staff. He was an Afro-Caribbean guy who used a wheelchair. I believe his reason for being in a wheelchair had to do with a crime. I also believe that the other inmates respected him, as did people on the outside. I don't know why staff had a problem with him. I think he was quite well off money-wise. Maybe the staff felt a hint of jealousy.

The staff in reception barely spoke to me the rest of that week. When they did, it was to call me or to tell me to put the kettle on. I was really unhappy, and I didn't know how to deal with it. If I reported any of them, then I would be classed as a grass and they would make my life at work more of a misery than it already was. But keeping my feelings inside and bottling them up was killing me.

One evening that week, I went to stand outside reception in the prison grounds just to get some air and get away from the dinosaurs. I remember that it was a really cold night, dark and eerie, and there were only dim lights lighting up where I was stood. I looked across the grounds. I could barely see a figure walking up towards where I was standing. It was the Catholic priest walking up from the prison church. His long, black robe was blowing in the wind and he was carrying a briefcase. There was no one else around, just him. It was like a scene from *The Exorcist*. I will never forget it. As he was approaching closer, I quickly thought that maybe I could talk to him and seek his advice. I knew that the vicars, priests, and the like were there for staff as well as for inmates. I was just about to walk towards the priest when a gust of wind came and lifted his robe right up over his head! All I could see were his white boxer shorts and his Dr Martens boots! It put me right off of speaking to him. Each time I saw him around the prison after that, I remembered this vision.

Christmas Eve arrived. Even though I was dreading going into work, I was on a high because I knew it was my last day before my annual leave for Christmas. When I got into work, I found that nearly all of the reception staff were in that day: Lester, Dan, Stef, Adam, and Karen. I could smell bacon frying in the staff kitchen. Karen said that Lester was in there making bacon sandwiches. I thought straightaway, "That's me. That's shit out, then." My co-workers were all standing in the main reception area. I went into the office to take off my coat.

Within a minute, Lester was shouting me. He had never shouted at me before, so I went out to where everyone else was standing. Lester said, "Here you go, a bacon sarny for you."

I was gobsmacked. I asked, "Is that really for me?"

He replied, "Yeah, and don't get fucking used to it. I have only made you one cos it's Christmas." I could not believe that he had actually made me a sandwich. Everyone else had a drink that Lester had made. There wasn't one for me, but I wasn't going to complain. I thought things were looking up. As I was eating my sandwich with the rest of the staff, I, for the first time since going into reception, felt like part of their team.

I wasn't aware of this at the time, but two staff members had come down to reception from the wings. They must have been in the staff kitchen making a brew. When they came into the main reception area, the male officer looked at me. He looked at Lester and said to him, "You didn't, did you?"

Lester busted up laughing and said, "I told you I was gonna do." The male officer then told me that Lester, earlier on, had picked up some bacon up that he had dropped on the floor, put it in a sandwich, and then said he was going to give it to the OSG. Everyone started laughing except for Adam, who walked off towards the prop room. Basically, that was why there was no drink for me. Lester had no intention of making me a sandwich or a drink. He dropped some bacon on the floor – which, by the way, was a very dirty floor – saw a situation which he thought he could use against me, and blagged me into thinking he had been nice because it was Christmas. I asked him why he would do such a dirty thing. He replied, "It was going spare, and I thought of you." What a tosser.

The wing staff who had come up to reception wanted some property cards photocopied, as the prison was conducting some random cell searches. I offered to do the photocopying for the wing staff. The photocopier was behind the main desk in reception. As I was doing the photocopying, Stef picked up a ruler, bent it back, and hit me on the backside with it. It made me jump more than anything. As I turned round to see who had done it, he laughed in my face and said, "What's up? Did that hurt?"

Then he did it again and again until I grabbed the ruler off him. I told him, "Yes, it did hurt, actually. Why don't you grow up?" The wing staff were still there and just looked at Stef as if he had gone out of his mind.

The time came when my shift finished. I just couldn't wait to get out of the prison. I knew I had a bit of time off, and I was very ready for it. As I left reception, I wished the staff a happy Christmas, but not one of them acknowledged me. When I got to my car, I sat and cried – and cried and cried. I don't know if it was my pure relief from knowing I was on leave or if it was because I was sad about everything that had happened over the past few weeks. I drove home. When I walked into my lovely home, I sat and cried again.

I had a lovely Christmas Day with my family, but when Christmas Day was over, I began to worry about going back to work – and I still had a week's annual leave left. That night as I was getting undressed in my bedroom, my husband walked into the bedroom and said, "What the hell is all that on your backside?" I looked over my shoulder into the mirror and saw that one side of my backside was covered in bruises. It was obvious to me that the bruises came from Stef's whacking me with the ruler. I told my husband what had happened, and he went mad. I then told him everything that had been going on in reception over the last few days. He knew I had been getting grief from the staff in reception, but when I told him about the bacon sandwich incident and how rude and impolite the staff had been, he was devastated. He told me I should report it, saying that I couldn't continue working under those circumstances. I explained to Bruce, my husband, that if I made a complaint or reported the officers, then they would make my life more of a misery than it already was.

During my annual leave, I was in contact with Eve, with whom I had worked in the works department. She knew I was having a bad time, so she and her husband, Adam, came to visit me at home. They both said I should do something about the situation, that I should report the officers' bad behaviour, but I told them both that I didn't want any repercussions. Adam asked if I would go back to the works department. He said I was missed there. Maybe if I asked my former manager about getting my former job back, he could sort something out for me to return. I didn't really have to think about it. I had moved to the reception to try to better myself in the Prison Service, but I was very unhappy there. Eve said that once she got back to work, as both she and Adam were on leave too, she would go speak with her manager and see what she could do.

My leave passed. It was the night before I was due back at work. My leave had been terrible, really. I hadn't been sleeping very well. Also, I noticed that I had started to get bald patches on my head. My hair had started to fall out. When I was getting my uniform ready in my bedroom for the following morning, I just broke down in tears. I sat on my bed, and I sobbed and sobbed. Bruce came into the bedroom, as my youngest daughter had told him she could hear me crying. He sat with me and didn't even ask why I was crying, as he was fully aware what was wrong. He reminded me that Eve was going to see if there was any chance of my returning to the works department. Hopefully, something would come of that, Bruce said. The thought that I may not be in reception for much longer cheered me up a little.

I returned to work the following day. Once again, I sat in the car park, not wanting to go inside. I could see my friends from the works department making their way into the prison. I envied them very much, as they all looked happy and were sharing conversations with each other. I didn't have that anymore. I got myself together, went into the prison, and made my way to reception. Most of the staff were in, and it was the same old. None of them acknowledged me. A little after I arrived, Adam, who works in reception, came in. Once again, he was the only one who spoke to me. He asked how my Christmas had been and then asked if I was OK. He was very nice to me. But to the rest of them, it was as if I didn't exist.

At lunchtime, I went down to the works department to see Eve in order to find out if she had had any joy with Mr H. She told me that she had been to see him but that there was nothing he could do, as there were no places available. She didn't tell him that I was having a hard time in reception. Rather, she had just asked if there was any chance of my returning. I don't know why, but I got a feeling that Eve was quietly pleased that I couldn't return to the works department. She seemed to have a little smirk on her face when she told me the news. I was gutted. It was a brand new year, January 2009, and I had nothing to look forward to in the Prison Service. It seemed as if I was going to be stuck in reception with a bunch of self-righteous, sexist, ignorant, prehistoric officers. My outlook on my career was dismal.

I returned to reception after I had finished my lunch. The first thing Stef said was, "You're fucking late again." I wasn't late. In all my time I worked at the prison, I was never once late. I always prided myself on my punctuality. I ignored Stef and went to look at the afternoon rota. I was on visits. I enjoyed doing visits. It was very easy to do, but I had to have my wits about me when I did this job. It was a matter of watching what went on between inmates and visitors. While I was in there that afternoon, I was sitting very close to the inmate who had had his chocolates stolen and other things stolen or taken from him. I really wanted to approach him and tell him what the staff had done, but it would have caused havoc, so I kept my mouth shut.

I returned to reception after I was finished with visits. There was no one around, so I went into the prop room to do some checks. About twenty minutes later, I heard Dan's voice. He was talking to another officer. I didn't recognise the second voice. I believe it must have been an officer from the wings. I heard the entire conversation the two men had. It was about an inmate who had asked them to help him get sprung. Apparently, the inmate had offered them two grand if they would help him. They were actually contemplating doing this. They were discussing how they could change entries in the diary so that they could be the escorting officers when the inmate had a hospital appointment. In the end, Dan must have bottled out (thank goodness). I listened carefully and remembered the date the two men were talking about. No prisoner's escape happened on that day. Like I said, Dan bottled out of it. Still, I couldn't believe that he had actually contemplated helping an inmate abscond. He didn't know I had been in the prop room – out of sight, out of mind, obviously. But I heard some startling things in the conversations the two were having. I waited until they had finished slagging off half of their colleagues before I went back out to the office. Dan then realised that I had appeared from somewhere. I saw the worry on his face, as if he were wondering where I had come from, wondering if I had heard his conversation with the other officer. He approached me and asked what I had been doing. I told him I had been in the prop room. I couldn't say anything else, really, because I wouldn't have lied and also because he could have checked the logs I had just done and worked out where I had been. He then threatened me. It was quite a scary threat, to be honest. And it worked for him, because it has taken me until now to speak up about the little conversation he had that day in reception.

After I went home that night, I was in a real state, not so much over what I had heard (I never thought for a minute that Dan and the other officer would spring some inmate), but over the fact that Dan had threatened me. I didn't even tell my husband that he had threatened me because I thought that would have caused a war. Bruce would not have been able to keep quiet about that. But he knew I was very upset. I told him that Eve had not had any joy with Mr H regarding my going back to the works department. He was gutted for me. I told him that I didn't know how long I could put up with working in reception.

The next few nights, I didn't sleep very well. I looked shocking. I was tired and I had bags under my eyes. My hair was falling out. I was in a terrible state. My husband began to see how much my job was affecting me and how much impact it was having on me.

A week or so later, I was in reception doing my normal duties – doing prop checks, standing at my post, being ignored, and so forth – when I got a call on my radio from someone asking if I would go to the works department ASAP to see Mr H. I wondered for a moment what Mr H could want with me, then I suddenly thought that he may have a position for me back in the works department. I went into my office and said to Lester, "I have just had a call on my radio to attend the works department, I won't be long."

He looked at me very nastily and said, "You are going fucking nowhere, girl. Go on your own time." He wasn't even my boss! But I thought to myself that if I went, he would just cause me grief. Seeing that it was only half an hour until my lunchtime, I waited and then went to the works department on my lunch break.

When I got into Mr H's office, he told me to sit down and asked me if I wanted a drink. He was being very nice, but he was always nice, so it was nothing out of the ordinary. He asked me how I was. I said I was OK. He asked me again, and I repeated that I was OK. He then looked at me with a very concerned look and said, "Oh, I see. So it is OK to be bullied?"

I said, "I have no idea what you are talking about."

He shook his head and said, "Look, I don't for one minute think it is OK for officers to ignore you, be rude to you, ask you to come to work in stockings and suspenders, hit you and bruise you, treat you bad because you are a woman, lock you in rooms, swear at you, and constantly make your life a misery." I was shocked and tried to think quickly who had told Mr H about these things. Was it Eve or Adam? Was it Adam from reception? I asked Mr H how he knew. He said to me, "Your husband is very concerned about you, and he has every right to be. And I am disappointed that you have not come to me before now." At that moment, I had many different thoughts. I felt like running out of Mr H's office, leaving the prison, going home, and smacking my husband in the face. Then I felt a bit relieved that things were now out in the open. Then I was scared. Then I was upset. I had many things going on in my head. So I told Mr H that it was all true and that I found working in reception to be a nightmare. Then I pleaded with him not to say anything. I asked him if there was any way at all that I could return to the works department and just forget that I had ever worked in reception. Mr H explained to me that it was his duty to report the bullying to the correct people. He said that because he was now aware of the situation, it was his duty to report it, not just because I was a former colleague of his, but also because, in general, if one hears of another being bullied or of any wrongdoing going on within the prison, then it is one's duty to report it. I tried saying to Mr H that I would get bullied even more once my colleagues' actions were reported. He tried to reassure me that I would be looked after and that the matter would be sorted. He said that he could not believe what had been happening and that I had not said anything to anyone about it. He told me to go back to reception and carry on as usual for the rest of my shift. In the meantime, he was going to go through the correct channels to set the wheels in motion. He said that he was deeply sorry that this had happened to me. He was even more deeply sorry that he did not have a place for me in the works department, as he had no places coming up.

Returning to reception, I was shaking like a leaf. No one asked where I had been, but I felt like they knew. They couldn't have known so quickly, but I was a dithering wreck. I just wanted my shift to end so I could get out of there. I kept myself to myself that day. When my shift ended, I got out of the prison as soon as I could. When I got home, I found Bruce in the kitchen with my brother Willie. I looked at Bruce and asked, "What the hell have you done?"

Before Bruce could answer, Willie said to me, "He is a more diplomatic man than me, because, to be honest, I want to go down there and wait outside the prison for the scum that have put you through this. And why the hell have you not told me?"

I replied, "For that reason alone."

So apparently, what I had undergone at work had gotten the better of Bruce. He had seen me suffer enough. His thoughts had been originally the same as Willie's. He wanted to go and confront the officers themselves, but he knew it would not turn out well. So earlier that morning, Bruce had been working across from the prison and saw Adam from the works department outside. Adam was escorting some contractors out of the prison. Bruce had gone over to speak to Adam, and Adam told him that I was being treated badly. He said that if it were his wife, then he would have to do something about it. As Bruce and Adam were talking, Mr H was walking out of the prison and going towards the car park. Adam pointed him out to Bruce and told him that he was my former manager. Bruce approached Mr H, introduced himself, and asked if he could have a word with him. Mr H was horrified when Bruce told him what had been going on. Bruce asked again if there was any way that I could return to the works department. He also told Mr H that I was afraid of reporting my co-workers' behaviour because of the consequences. Mr H told Bruce that he would call me in and speak to me.

The morning after this, I got up to go to work, but I couldn't go in to work. I had not slept, I was crying, I was dreading the unknown, and I was a total wreck. I phoned in to Karen and told her that I was under the weather and wouldn't be coming in. She said to keep her informed about how I was. She never mentioned anything regarding the previous day's happenings, so I presumed she had not been informed. I went to the doctor's, and the doctor put me straight onto sickness leave. I was suffering with stress, sleep deprivation, and alopecia.

On the following morning, Karen contacted me and told me that someone from human resources had told her that I had been the victim of bullying. On the phone, she sounded very concerned and asked if I would meet her in a neutral meeting place away from the prison. We arranged to meet the following day in Café Nero at lunchtime. The first thing she did upon seeing me the next day was put her arms around me and give me a massive hug. Once we were inside the café, she ordered coffee for the both of us. I basically had to tell her all that had been going on. She said that part of her was shocked and part of her was expecting it. She tried blaming herself for not being there when I first started in reception, but again she kept on saying that she was aware of the officers being bullies, especially Lester. She told me that Lester had been accused many a time in the past of bullying other staff and inmates. I wondered why the hell he was still there.

Karen said that the officers play a game against each other to see who can be the meanest, toughest officer. It was as if she was making excuses for their behaviour. She also said that Lester hated the fact that she was a senior officer and was higher ranked than he was. She did come across as being upset about what had happened to me. She asked me why I didn't go to her first. I told her that I didn't want to tell anyone because I didn't want any repercussions. I also told her that it was my husband who had spoken to Mr H and that it was Mr H who had actually made the report. She told me that she would have to pass the information on to her manager. After that, she said that she would contact me in the next day or two and inform me of what would happen next.

The following day, Karen contacted me and said that Darren, the PO from reception, would be coming to my house the following day to conduct an interview. This was the same Darren who had been out on that night out when I was with my former colleagues, the one who was blathered drunk, coming on to Adam's wife, Eve, and slagging off all the OSGs. Nice. Darren came to my house the following day and conducted an interview. He took down all the details of what had been happening. He said that I should have gone to someone earlier and made a complaint. I gave him my reasons why I hadn't done this. He kept saying that the officers in reception were very strong characters and were set in their ways. I told him that this did not excuse their behaviour towards me. He explained that he would go back to the prison and interview each officer individually. Once he had done this, he would take his findings to Governor Number One and would get back to me with the outcome. He did ask me if I would consider going back to work in reception. I laughed at him and asked him, "Would you?"

He replied, "No, of course not."

My husband came home when Darren was almost done with the interview. For some reason, Darren started stuttering and stammering when Bruce came in. He seemed to turn into a dithering wreck. He told Bruce that he had done the right thing by bringing the matter to Mr H's attention, as the prison wouldn't allow bullying in the workplace. Bruce and I didn't realise it at the time, but because of the allegations being made – bullying, sexual harassment, and so forth – Darren should not have come alone to conduct the interview. He should have had an accompanying female member of staff with him. However, I recorded the interview for my own benefit. Bruce and I were aware that Darren would go write up what had been said, but we decided that we needed a recording in case anything different from what actually took place was claimed. Bruce and I had researched the use of recordings. Our findings were that recordings may be used if necessary at a later date if all parties agree to it.

Within a few days, Darren contacted me and asked if I would return to the prison and meet with him so he could explain what would happen next. This I did. I was dreading going back into the prison, but I had to do it. Darren came to meet me in the search area and then took me straight up to his office. He explained that he had conducted all the interviews with the staff from reception. The three main culprits, Lester, Dan, and Stef, denied all of the allegations. This was expected. Karen had said that she knew something was wrong but did not realise just how bad things were for me. Darren then explained that the three officers, Lester, Dan, and Stef, had received a verbal warning and had been put on report. He said that the complaint had been left open and would remain in Governor Number One's office in case of any repercussions. The officers would remain in reception, and I had to move out. I was glad that the officers had been given a verbal warning and that the matter had been left with Governor Number One. I was quietly despondent that I was the one who had to move out of reception, however. I had done nothing wrong, yet I was the one who had to leave the job that I originally thought would get me on the ladder within the Prison Service. However, my overall thoughts were that I did not have to work with and tolerate those nasty people anymore. So my next question was, "Where do I go now?" Darren said that my name was back down for a place at the works department. In the meantime, the PO in the gate area to whom Darren had spoken would find duties for me. He then told me to go home and report next morning to the gate area, where they would have a rota made up for me.

The following morning, I went into the prison, reported in the gate area, and went to see what duties I had been given. I couldn't believe it: they had put me on staff search. There was no one there for me to speak to, so I had to go straight into the search area. Within the first five minutes of my being on search, there they were, all three of them: Lester, Dan, and Stef. They purposely waited so they could all come through my portal together. The other OSG who was on the other portal told them to go through his portal, but they refused, saying they wanted to come through mine. Not one of them said a word to me, but the looks they gave me were terrifying. I had to rub each one of them down and conduct a search on them. It was awful.

I went to get my bag and coat. I left the prison and went home. As soon as I got home, Bruce phoned Darren and went ballistic. Darren said that he had no idea that I had been put on staff search. He admitted that staff search should have been the last place for me to work. Bruce asked Darren how he would have felt had it been his wife in my place. Darren said he would not have put up with it and would have done exactly the same thing. He couldn't apologise enough after he admitted that the gate area was a hostile area for me to work.

Later that day, Darren contacted me and said that a place had come up in the works department. I could go back there the following day. This just shows that things can be put in place. My husband has this saying, "He who shouts the loudest gets heard." It always made me laugh, that saying did, but that day it had worked.

I was overwhelmed. I was going back to work with people who were nice. I was no longer bothered about gaining a promotion. If becoming an officer turns a person into an animal like the ones in reception, then an OSG I would remain.

Back in the Works Department

I was very happy going into work on the following day. I went straight to Mr H's office. He welcomed me back with open arms. I thanked him very much for sorting it for me. He explained to me that it was actually Dick, the assistant manager, who had sorted it for me. I went straight to see Dick and thanked him. He told me that one of the OSGs, Charles, had gotten the fire officer's job but couldn't leave until there was a replacement for him. Dick, knowing that the prison was desperate for Charles to take the fire officer's job, was fully aware that I was desperate to return to the works department, so he rushed the paperwork through. And there I was. There was a lot of paperwork to be done that day. Darren had to release me from the reception, which was the best feeling ever. Mr H had to release Charles from the works department. After that, I was formally set, back in the works department. Darren told me that I would be exempt from ever working in the gate area because I had been bullied there and it was now a hostile area for me. The only times I had to go through the gate area were literally when I arrived at the prison at the beginning of my shift and when I was preparing to depart at the end of my shift.

I later returned to the works department. All of my colleagues cheered when I walked in the office. It was one of the best feelings ever. Mitch was really happy that I had returned. As I mentioned before, as soon as I met Mitch, I knew he would become a good friend. Everyone was talking about how I had been treated in reception. Even though they were all glad to have me back, they thought it unfair that I, not those who bullied me, was the one who had to leave reception. But it didn't matter to me anymore. I was happy again. I was going be content, not unhappy, in the workplace. That meant the world to me.

Over the next few weeks, I got back into the swing of things. There were a few occasions when I was in or around the prison and I saw the officers from reception. They glared at me and talked amongst themselves when they saw me, like little schoolgirls. But my colleagues always backed me up and were there for me. Even the contractors gave me their backing.

One day, Eve and I got a call to go up to the contractors search area in order to pick up some contractors who had just arrived in the prison. Contractors search was joined to the reception and was very close to the place where vehicles came into and went out of the prison. As Eve and I were approaching the contractors search, I could see that a Category A wagon had just entered the prison. The speed limit was 5 mph around the prison, for obvious reasons. Eve had just stepped onto the path from the roadway. I was behind her and was approaching the path. All of a sudden, the Category A wagon sped up and was coming straight towards me. I had to literally jump out of its way and onto the path. Eve grabbed me, as I was unsteady on my feet. She said, "Are you OK? Fucking hell, you must have a death wish!" We waited purposely to see who got out of the wagon. It was Lester. He didn't even look at us. He looked the other way. Eve told me to go report the incident, but I didn't want to. I'd had enough of that in the past and didn't want to cause a stir.

When we got back down to the works department, Eve told the rest of the team what Lester had done. They went mad, telling me I had to report it straightaway. They said that my complaint had been left open for this reason alone. Also, they said that it would all be on camera and that Eve was a witness, so what would I have to lose – and what could Lester try doing next time to me?

So Eve and I went up to see Darren, the PO from reception. We both told him exactly what had happened. His reaction was, "When will Lester ever fucking learn? What a fucking knobhead!" He said he would go up to the control room, get the incident up on camera, pull Lester in, and ask him what he was doing. I didn't hear anything about the matter over the next few days, but I saw Lester a couple of times. He just smirked at me. My colleagues told me to go see Darren again and find out what had been done, so I did. Darren told me that there had been a fault on that particular camera that day and nothing was showing up. What a crock of shit. Very important cameras in a top-security prison don't experience faults. The cameras are backed up and are constantly checked throughout the day and night. In my opinion, and also in my colleagues' opinion, this was a cover-up so Lester wouldn't have to answer for what he had done. That incident was brushed under the carpet.

The following weeks and months were great in the works department. I and my co-workers got on really well as a team. We did our jobs well, went on training days together, and had nights out together. If problems arose, we would help one another. In the summer of that year, we arranged a weekend away to Sunderland. Some of the contractors whom we escorted at the prison came from Sunderland. They invited all of us there to go out with them, so we made a weekend of it. We all booked into a hotel and organised a minibus. It was a great weekend. We all ended up worse for wear, but it was a really good time, something we thoroughly enjoyed.

When I and my co-workers went into work on the Monday morning after our weekend away, we discovered that we had all received a memo from Dick out of the works department saying that we had breached prison rules by accepting bribes from the contractors. We were all clueless and gobsmacked about this. So we went up to the works department to ask what the accusation was all about. Dick said that he believed that the contractors had paid for our hotel rooms, our minibus, and the drinks we consumed in exchange for information about inmates. He said that if we couldn't prove any different, we would all face disciplinary measures and the contractors would be thrown off the job. This was absolutely absurd. Basically, my colleagues and I could not have a night out with people whom we had gotten to know over the past few months without it looking like we were all accepting bribes. Unbelievable. So, we all had to retrieve our hotel bookings from the Internet, print them out, get confirmation of the minibus booking, and take these documents into the prison, all to prove our innocence. The only thing we could not prove was that we had bought our own drinks. The prison accepted the documents as proof of our innocence, much to Dick's disappointment.

A week or so after this incident, Mr H needed someone to work two weeks on the night shift with some contractors who were doing a deep clean of the inmates' kitchen. For obvious reasons – because the kitchen is used throughout the day – this job could only be done during the night. None of our team wanted to do it, as it can be a bit of a nightmare working at night in the prison. This is because one is not allowed keys during the night, so, wherever one is, he or she has to remain there until the following morning. There is no chance of going anywhere or just bobbing into the grounds to take a break or anything like that. None of this bothered me, so I offered to do these night shifts.

The following week came. My night shifts began. At this time, the prison was holding a very high-profile inmate who was on trial. The security for him was immense. When he left the prison on a morning, armed police would be there and the police helicopter would be hovering. The same applied upon his return to the prison in the evenings. It cost millions of pounds for the trial and for the security measures that had to be taken. The inmate was very dangerous. When he was brought back to the prison in the evenings, no one was allowed to enter or leave the prison until the armed guard had gotten him back inside. The same applied on a morning.

When my night shifts started, I had arrived at work and was going into the prison around the same time of the inmate's evening return. Once I was inside, I had to wait for my contractors to arrive and get through the search area. The first night they arrived, they were a little late, as it was their first time at this prison and they had presumably gotten lost on the way. They were a good set of lads, polite and talkative. Also, they adhered to the rules that were in place. They were OK. One of them, who was the driver of the van, was a little bit slow on the uptake, but he was still a good guy.

I got the contractors down to the kitchen and explained to them that they were in there for the full night and couldn't go anywhere else around the prison. They were OK with this in general, although they were devastated that they couldn't go out for a smoke.

I explained to the contractors about the high-profile inmate being on trial. I had to make them aware, as they would be arriving in the evening around the same time when the inmate was getting back from court. I told them that on some nights they may have to wait outside the prison until the armed guard left. They were fine about it.

The night went well, but there was nowhere for me to sit. I found myself leaning against a steel worktop all night. By 3 a.m., I was aching a lot and could feel myself wanting to fall asleep where I stood. I couldn't wait to get home and go to bed.

The following night, I went into the prison and was standing and waiting for my contractors inside at the very front of the prison. The gate staff had gotten a call saying the high-profile inmate was on his way back and to be on alert for his arrival. A few minutes later, the first of the armed police arrived. Shortly afterwards, the van carrying the inmate arrived. I was talking to some of the search staff when one of them asked me, "Liz, are they your contractors driving up?"

I looked out and noticed their old, blue van driving up towards the prison. "Yes," I replied. The armed police had raised their arms to tell my contractors to stop, but for some reason they continued driving up towards the prison.

I heard one of the staff say, "Oh, good God, what the hell?" I looked out again and saw that the armed police had dragged all three of my contractors out of their van. The police had them lying flat on the ground, face down, their arms and legs spread. The contractors were in the middle of the road with guns pointing at their heads! It was like a scene from *The Sweeney*. My contractors made it into the prison about ninety minutes later. The driver was still crying! The other two were still in shock. They couldn't concentrate on their work properly for that entire night. It was quite funny, really. The incident was all they could talk about all night long. They had been proper scared. I reminded them that I had previously told them about this matter, but they seemed oblivious and said that they presumed they had priority as they were the kitchen cleaners. Ha.

During that night, a senior officer (SO) named Patrick came into the kitchen to see how we all were doing. I knew him. He used to see a friend of mine until things went pear-shaped between them, but I still thought he was a really nice fella. He asked me why I was leaning on the worktop and not sitting in the senior officer's office. I told him the office was locked up and I didn't have keys. He said, "Well, it must be unlocked, because the kitchen senior officer said that he had left you a note on his desk." Patrick went to check the door and said, "Typical of Darren, this. Leaves you a note on his desk, then locks the office door so you can't get in. Excellent."

I didn't know who Darren was, but Patrick said that Darren was one of a kind. I soon came to realise this when I went into the office and saw the note he had left. It read, "Hello, OSG Liz and contractors. Help yourselves to any of the food in the fridges and storeroom, but don't touch my fucking Danish bacon or I'll have to kill you."

Patrick just looked at me and asked, "See what I mean?" Then he told me to sit in the office instead of perching on the edge of a worktop.

He said he would keep bobbing in to see if we needed anything. I thought he was a really nice guy. I kept looking at the note that Darren had left on the desk. Each time I read it, I had a little giggle.

The night shifts went OK. At the end of the first week, I saw that Darren had left another note on his desk. This one read, "OSG Liz, please tell your contractors to turn the fucking radio down during the night. The cons can't sleep and have put in a complaint." So I told the contractors about this. They turned the radio down straightaway, bless them. I think having the radio on during the night helps the night go quicker and helps one to stay awake, but in all fairness the contractors did have it a little loud.

The second week went by pretty quick. The high-profile inmate was still on trial, and all the security and armed guard were still in place. About halfway through one particular night, the contractors was talking about the high-profile inmate. They had googled him apparently and were talking about his crimes and how dangerous he was. He wasn't a paedophile or a rapist. I believe he was the gangster type and had a lot of influence and a lot of fingers in a lot of pies. I believe he was the kind that if he asked you for a chip, you would give him your fish. So the contractors were talking on and off all night about him. They seemed mesmerised about him. A little later that night, we all sat together to eat our pack-ups. The contractor who was a bit slow on the uptake realised he had left his pack-up in the van. The van was in the prison grounds, but we couldn't get to it, as I had no keys to get me around the prison. The other two contractors were ribbing the third for forgetting his snap. I felt sorry for him and offered to share my pack-up with him, but he didn't want to. I could see he felt awkward. So I said to him, "Look, the SO left a note saying we could eat any food out of the fridges or the storeroom as long as we didn't eat the Danish bacon, so go have a look about and get something to eat." This he did. I didn't notice what it was he had found to eat. I think he had made some kind of sandwich and salad or something. He said he had thoroughly enjoyed it, mentioning that it was different from what he usually ate.

The following morning, the contractors had gotten all packed up and were ready to leave for the day. We had to be out of the kitchen before 6 a.m., as the inmates and the staff who worked in the kitchen had to be in at that time to start making the breakfasts. For some reason, the prison was at a standstill on this particular morning. There must have been an incident somewhere in the prison. When there was an incident, whether it was a fire alarm, a kick-off between inmates, a roll countdown, or some other happening, the prison would come to a standstill. No one would be allowed to move until the incident was over. Then there would have to be a full count. This could take ages, but there was nothing anyone could do about it. So I explained to the contractors that we would just have to be patient and wait. Laurel, the high-profile inmate, would still have to be taken out though, as it was scheduled for him every day, and it took a lot of time, money, and planning.

The contractors and I were still stuck in the kitchen at around 7.15 a.m. when a different senior officer came into the kitchen to tell us that the standstill would be soon over. He had come into the kitchen for another reason too: to collect Laurel's packed lunch for court. Apparently, Laurel had special requirements for his diet, so every evening a special pack-up would be made for him for the following day, as the court couldn't provide the food he required. If Laurel didn't get his special diet, he would kick off, as he believed that the special food was vital to his well-being. So I think you may have guessed what happened next. The SO went to the fridges to find that the prepared pack-up was gone. My contractor had eaten it. The SO came to me and asked me where it was. I had to come clean and tell him what had happened. I explained that the contractor had forgotten his pack-up and that SO Darren had left a note about us having some food. Nothing I said, however, seemed to soften the blow. The contractor culprit was all of a sudden dumbstruck. I could see the fear on his face. I asked the SO if there was something else we could make or put together for Laurel. Ironically, the kitchen was awaiting a new delivery of special dietary foods that day and had used the very last of them on the previous day for Laurel. The SO said he would try to sort it with Laurel. He let us go once the standstill had come to an end. When I was escorting the contractors out of the prison, the contractor in question said that he wasn't going to be back that night, that he was going to throw a sickie. His pals told him to stop being a wussy and to get a grip.

The following night was actually our last night in the kitchen. The job was almost complete, and the contractors required only a few hours to get it finished. On my arrival to the kitchen, I went straight into the SO's office. He had left a note again. It read, "OSG Liz, please tell the contractor who is responsible for eating Laurel's lunch that Laurel has now put a hit on him. Laurel has stipulated that whichever way his trial goes, guilty or not, the contractor that took his food had better sleep with one eye open." I knew that this was just a wind-up from SO Darren, but the contractor saw the note and couldn't get out of the prison quickly enough. All three of them were done and dusted before midnight that night. When SO Paddy came in to see us, we asked if we could have permission to leave the prison, as the job was complete. Paddy sorted this for us, so we had an early finish that night. On leaving the prison, the contractors all shook my hand and said that they had loved working with me. I said I would see them six months later when they were due again for the deep clean. But they were all in agreement that they would be sending different contractors in. I wonder why?

I returned to the works department the following week. My colleagues had all missed me. My relationship with Mitch started to flourish at this time. We became really good friends, as we were very much alike. We liked to do our jobs to the best of our ability, and we were always the two who would work over when extra man-hours were required. It was compulsory that when contractors needed to work over, someone from our team had to work over with them. There were twelve of us on the team at that time, but I could count on one hand how many would volunteer to work over. And if ever there would be a time when no one wanted to work over, then our manager would literally draw names from a bag. This didn't happen often, as I or Mitch often volunteered. It was good to work over though, because we were required to work only three or four hours during those times. We would either get paid time and a half or use the time as toil. Toil consisted of taking off the same amount of hours as the hours one worked over. Mitch and I could let our toil build up. Before we knew it, we had three or four days' extra leave to take. Mitch and I didn't mind working over at all. Because of this, we spent a lot of time together, Mitch and I, and, as I said, became very good friends.

After Mr H retired, we in the works department had a new manager: Dick, who was previously Mr H's assistant manager. It was a sad day when Mr H left. He was such a good man. Everyone in my department went to a local pub to have a leaving party for him. The governor from our department, Mr P, was also in attendance at the leaving party. He stared at my legs all night. The following day at work, I asked our

Governor P if had had a good night. He replied, "Well, I couldn't stop staring at your beautiful legs, so, yes, I had a lovely night, my dear." He said this in front of half of my colleagues, so after that it was always a stand-up joke about our governor fancying my legs, ha!

Once Dick became our manager, things changed a little bit in the works department. We didn't see major changes, but maybe we had been spoilt by having Mr H as our manager. Mr H was very fair and would not take any crap off anyone. He always showed diplomacy and treated us all as equals. He was looking forward to his retirement. I do hope he is enjoying it and living life to the full.

Not very long after Dick became our manager, we got two new starters in our department, Dane and Keith. Keith wasn't a new starter in the prison. He had worked in the control room for many years, but he had left the control room and was working with the yard party (the binmen) while he awaited a place with us. Dane was a new starter in the prison. He had worked in the gate area for a short while, but he wasn't well liked, so they moved him out and sent him to us. Dane was only a young lad, about nineteen. According to the gate staff, he came to the prison with a know-it-all attitude. They said that during his training, Dane stated that he didn't need to do control and restraint training, as he could handle any inmate who might come at him. That went down like a lead balloon with the training staff. But I never listened to rumours about people. I would not judge anyone by other people's opinions. So when Dane joined us, I treated him the same as I would treat anyone else. However, some of the lads in our team immediately had nothing down for him. Neither did Eve. She never once spoke to him. It was as if she had had a long-time grudge against him, yet she hadn't met him prior to his joining our department. I asked Dane where he lived and what he had done before he joined the Prison Service. I found out that he lived in the village next to mine and had gone to the same school as my daughters had. I never mentioned my daughters' names to him; I just said that they went to the same school.

When I got home that night, I was telling my middle daughter about this new starter we had, saying that he must have gone to her school. When she asked his name and I answered, she informed me that Dane was her first boyfriend. I never knew this because it was just a bit of a school-age boyfriend–girlfriend kind of thing and they only used to meet up after school on the playing field behind our house. Their relationship didn't last very long before it phased out. But what a small world. The following day, I told Dane who my daughter was. He said he couldn't believe it. Then he told me that he still carried a flame for her, but he thought he wasn't good enough for her now. So Dane and I had a common denominator, my daughter.

The majority of the people on our team didn't like Dane, and a few of them made their feelings quite clear to him and to everyone else. I felt this was a bit unfair, as Dane had never done anything wrong to any of them. Before long, they began to make his life a misery. He tolerated it for some time, but he had me and Mitch to talk to. None of the others would work with him. Others on the team would ask me or Mitch to swap partners so that Dane would end up working with one of us two. We did this because we felt sorry for Dane. Plus, we didn't mind working with him at all.

During the following weeks, the OSG who was sort of in charge of the compound, Drew, became very despondent in his role. He became very moody and miserable and stopped taking responsibility for his duties. The rest of us didn't know why he became this way, but we all noticed it, especially Adam and Eve. Adam then started to get at Drew, often having a go at him, calling him out, and just basically making his life a misery. Things got worse. There was a bad atmosphere every day at work. In the end, Drew went to see our manager, Dick, and made a complaint against Adam. Drew didn't want any repercussions, so he asked Dick if something could be done about Adam but without Dick's bringing Drew's name into it. This was quite a difficult situation for Dick. I believe that Dick put Adam on the rota to work outside the prison with the outside contractors, determining that he would monitor the situation. I think that after a day or two, Adam and Eve clicked on to what was happening. I think they were aware that Drew had made a complaint, but they couldn't prove it. So things got worse for Drew. Drew got more depressed, and everyone else became miserable. It then got to the stage where some of the team saw this situation as an "I'll do what I want" kind of thing. They began to take advantage of the situation. For example, because Drew stopped taking responsibility for being in charge, some of the team sat in the office all day and refused to go out to escort contractors. This job was therefore left to the likes of me and Mitch and a few others. Drew would not intervene and tell the staff that they weren't pulling their weight. He simply continued losing interest in his role. Adam continued to make Drew unhappy. Drew confided in me and Mitch, saying that he wanted to go back to escorting the contractors and not be in charge anymore. He said the job had become too much for him and he couldn't handle the responsibility. Plus, there was about to be more work and more contractors, as the prison had just sealed a massive contract. A motion to build a new kitchen had been passed. It was going to be a massive job.

The following day, Mitch and I were up in the estates building, which is where all the bosses' offices were situated. Dick our manager, Mr P our governor, and the administrative staff for the works department were all housed in the estates building. Mitch and I had gone up to pick up some men from the home office and escort them around the prison to view where the new building was going to be situated. Once we escorted them around and then taken them back to the estates, Drew asked Mitch and me to come in his office. He asked us what the problem was down in the compound. He told us that Drew had made a complaint against Adam. He knew that things weren't right. Mitch and I didn't say anything about Adam's behaviour towards Drew, but we did say that Drew wasn't happy, that he was wanting to go back to escorting, and that he didn't want to be in charge anymore. Well, with that, Dick asked if Mitch and I would be in charge of the compound and the contractors. He explained that the prison would soon require two staff to be in charge because of the new contract. He thought that Mitch and I were the most responsible people to be in charge. He would then put Drew back escorting as Drew had wished. He told Mitch and me to go away and think about it and to let him know our decision within the next day or two. I, knowing that it was a huge responsibility to be in charge, was quite honoured to have been asked by Dick. I believe that Mitch felt the same way. Plus, it is always a good thing to have on your CV when you have been in charge of a department in the Prison Service. So Mitch and I both decided in favour of being in charge. It was all put in place. Within a week, Drew was back to escorting, and Mitch and I had taken over the compound.

While being in charge, I saw more of what was going on between the team members. I also saw how much Dane was getting picked on. Dane was quite overweight at that time. He was actually on the NHS waiting list to have a gastric-band operation. The team members who didn't like him were constantly at him about his weight problem, even though they were all aware that it was a major problem for him. Adam was Dane's worst antagonist. This was very surprising to me, because Adam was twice the size of Dane. Adam was a very big bloke indeed, but his weight obviously didn't bother him the way that Dane's weight bothered Dane.

There were four on the team who began to bully Dane, Adam being the main culprit. They would tell him to start eating salads because he was a fat bastard (their words, not mine). They also told him he would never get a girlfriend because of his weight. They became vile towards him. Dane just ignored them most of the time, but I could see it was getting him down, as it would anyone.

Then one day while Mitch and I were doing a tool check in the tool store, we discovered that our lottery fund was missing. At that time, all our team members had a key to get in to the main gate leading to the works department. While Mitch and I were in the tool store, someone must have come into the compound and seized the opportunity to take the money. There were only three team members who had returned to the compound in that time: Tamwar, Drew, and Dane. Obviously, Mitch and I were in the compound too, so there were five of us who could have taken it. Dane got the blame from most of the team. People from the security department were involved. They came down and did a search, but to no avail. Thereafter, our manager, Dick, decided that only Mitch and I would be allowed to have keys to that gate. This made our jobs harder, as each time an escort or a contractor or a prison staff member came to the compound, either Mitch or I would have to go to let the person in. Mind you, there would be someone at the gate wanting to gain access almost all day long.

Dane was banished by most members of the team. Within a day, it was all round the prison that Dane had stolen our lottery fund, so other staff members were also giving Dane the cold shoulder. I still wouldn't like to speculate about what happened to the lottery fund, as there was never any evidence that Dane had taken it. Everyone was upset that the lottery fund had gone, as we saved it up all year. The plan was to divvy it up at Christmas. Normally, it was a nice little bonus for us at the end of the end of the year. I think that about £180 went missing.

A few days after the lottery incident, the contracts managers, the prison managers, and the officials from the home office were having a meeting. This occurred every week on a Thursday morning. One of the contracts managers would bring in snacks to have during the meeting – pork pies, sausage rolls, etc. If any of the snacks were left after the meeting, the manager would bring them down into our cabin and tell us to have them. Prior to the meeting, Dane had told me that he had left home that morning in a rush and had forgotten his lunch. Also, he had not picked up his wallet on his way out of the house. Basically, he had nothing to eat. I told him that if the contracts manager brought any snacks down later in the morning, then I would make sure I saved him some. Dane thanked me and went off escorting for the morning.

The contracts manager did come down just before lunch and brought what was left over from the meeting. On this particular day, not many people had attended the meeting, so there were absolutely loads of pies and sausage rolls. I think there were about ten of us on shift that day, and there was easily enough for a pie and a sausage roll for each for us – probably more, as Eve was a vegetarian. Well, she claimed to be, but she ate chicken and fish. So Mitch took a pie and a sausage roll, put them in a bag, and put them on my desk for when Dane came back for lunch. All the escorts returned around the same time for their lunch breaks except for Dane, who was still out somewhere on an escort. The escorts all started sharing the pies and rolls. Adam and another colleague, Kieran, were laughing at the thought that no one had saved any for Dane. Then Kieran saw the bag on my desk and asked me what was in it. I told him the bag was for Dane when he came in for lunch. Adam opened up the bag and asked if anyone wanted what was inside. Nobody wanted any more food. I said, "We've all had some, Adam. They are for Dane."

He said, "Fuck him. He is not getting any." I argued with Adam, saying that Dane had forgotten his lunch and, therefore, had nothing to eat – and that's why I had put this food to one side. Adam wasn't having any of it, and neither was Kieran. I heard the gate rattling. I knew it was Dane returning for his lunch. I went to unlock the gate. As I did so, Dane asked if there were any snacks left for him, to which I replied that I had put some aside for him. As he and I were approaching the cabin, Kieran was standing outside the cabin, throwing Dane's pie and sausage roll to the pigeons. I could hear the rest of the escorts laughing from inside the cabin. Dane walked into the cabin and asked what was funny. Adam said, "We're laughing at the fact that Kieran has just fed the pigeons with your snap."

Dane looked at me and asked, "Why would they do that?"

Before I could answer, Adam butted in and said, "Cos you are a fat bastard, Dane. You can do without, but the pigeons need feeding." All the escorts were in hysterics. Mitch and I couldn't see the funny side to this. It was cruel, really, what the staff had done. And if someone had done that to either Adam or Kieran, then there would have been hell to pay. Dane sat in the corner of the cabin and said nothing. I went into my snap box. Seeing that I had a chocolate bar and a bag of crisps, I handed them to Dane. He gratefully took them.

Again, Adam started to have a go, this time at me. "Why the fuck are you giving him your snap?" he asked me.

I replied, "Once again, he has no lunch. And you lot have tried to make sure that he doesn't have any. If I want to give him a chocolate bar and a bag of crisps, then I will."

The escorts began behaving worse and worse towards Dane. It got to the stage where Dane didn't want to come into work. He started using his annual leave and the toil hours that he had saved up. That wasn't right. When he had no more annual leave to use, he had no choice but to come in to work. The escorts were the same with him. One particular day at the end of shift, Dane had taken off his boots to enable him to remove his waterproofs. While he was removing his waterproofs, Tamwar took Dane's boots and threw them into a recycling bin. The recycling bin was one of those from which something couldn't be retrieved once it had been put in. That evening, Dane had to walk through the search area, leave the prison, and drive home with no boots on. I believe that that was the final nail in the coffin for him. The following morning when he came into work, he entered the prison through the search area. He collected his radio but did not come down to our department. Later that morning, I got a call on my radio asking if I could attend the estates department. This I did. Mitch covered the compound as up I went to the estates. When I got up there, I saw Dane sitting in a room on his own. As I was approaching the room, he beckoned me in. He told me that he couldn't take the bullying anymore and that he had reported it through the correct channels. He had not gone direct to our manager; instead, he had gone higher and had seen someone from HR. They had given him some forms to fill in, on which he had to name the people who had been bullying him. He said that once he took the forms back, he would go home. He was distraught.

I felt for him because his predicament reminded me of my time in reception. I could see what the bullying was doing to him. I could see the effect it was having on him.

The following day, Dane came into work. I could see that he was fearing the worst. He had reported the bullying and was dreading the consequences. Our manager, Dick, called Dane to his office. From what Dane told me afterwards, I know that he had had to make a formal complaint. Over the next few days, Adam, Kieran, Declan, and Tamwar were all called up to see Dick. They were all told that they had been accused of bullying. They would all have to give statements. Adam, once again, was the main culprit, like he had been with Kerry and like he had been with Drew. As you can imagine, this news went down like a lead balloon. But instead of continuing to bully Dane, the four OSGs totally ignored him, which is still a form of bullying – silent bullying. It made my and Mitch's job quite difficult, as all the escorts went on principle and refused point-blank to work with Dane. They didn't like working with him beforehand, but sometimes they had to. But now, it was just a mess. And obviously, the escorts accused of bullying were panicking and thinking about what might happen to them in regards to disciplinary action.

A couple of days later, there was quite a few of us in the cabin: me, Mitch, Dane, Adam, and one or two more. (I don't remember exactly who were present.) Dane asked me, "Liz, have you ever noticed that Dick is never here on a Tuesday?"

I thought for a minute and realised Dane was right. "Oh yes," I said. "I wonder why?"

Dane looked around the cabin and said, "I know why. He told me the other day when I went to see him in his office." Now I could see that this was killing Adam. He really wanted to know why Dick was never at work on a Tuesday but has he was not speaking to Dane, so he couldn't ask the question. So I asked Dane why. Dane replied, "I can't really tell anyone. I just wondered if you had noticed that he is never here on a Tuesday."

At that point, Adam stood up and said, "For fuck's sake, Dane, just tell us why Dick doesn't come in on a Tuesday!"

What Dane told us was such a shock. He said that when he was in Dick's office, he was quite upset about having to report the bullying and was also upset about some personal problems that he had at home. Dick had explained to Dane that he was not alone in enduring problems, that even Dick himself was having problems at home. Dick told Dane (in confidence) that his son had been taken into care for sexually abusing his younger sister (Dick's daughter). Dick mentioned that he took each Tuesday off to go visit his son. I found it quite a shock, the fact that our manager would tell a member of staff what was occurring with his son – and especially someone like Dane. No disrespect to Dane, but like I stated earlier, Dane was a young bloke with an attitude. I wouldn't particularly trust him with information that I didn't want anyone else to know. He proved this point by blurting out Dick's secret within a couple of days.

On top of his other admission to Dane, Dick apparently had said that the governor of the works department, Mr P, was unaware that Dick took Tuesday off each week. My thinking was that either Dane was just saying this stuff to somehow get Adam to speak to him again (which, if that were the case, worked) or that Dick was putting his trust in Dane. Well, to my astonishment, the truth turned out to be neither of those things. On the following Monday, when Adam, Kieran, Declan, and Tamwar were due for disciplinary action because of their bullying, Adam used this information for his own purposes. He went to see Dick first thing that morning and told him that he wanted a meeting with our governor, Mr P, as he had some information for him regarding a higher-ranked member of staff. When Dick asked Adam what it was about, Adam said it was something that Dane had been saying. Later that morning, Dick came especially to see me and asked me what I knew about why Adam had requested to see Mr P. I said that I was unsure. Dick said, "Oh, come on, Liz, you hear everything that gets said down here. Just tell me what Dane has said to Adam, cos I think it is about me."

So I said to Dick, "Well, if you haven't said anything untoward to Dane, then you have nothing to worry about."

Dick then said, "That's the problem, I have. I told Dane something personal in confidence, and I think he has blabbed." I just gave Dick the look of, "Why the hell would you do that?"

Lo and behold, before Adam got the chance to meet with Mr P, Dick called the four staff members who had been accused of bullying to his office and told them that no further action would be taken. He asked them if they would lay off of Dane. And that was it; the bullying issue was over. Of course, Adam, Kieran, Declan, and Tamwar didn't lay off Dane, seeing as they had a licence to bully and get away with it.

Not long after this occurrence, Dane was involved in an incident outside of the prison. I believe that it was some kind of fighting incident. Even though it was an incident outside of the prison, Dane received a letter from Governor Number One terminating his employment with the Prison Service. But the governor had stated that the reason for Dane's termination of employment was that his actions outside the prison were immature. As a result, he had brought the prison into disrepute. And that is where Dane had gotten the governor. Dane and his solicitor travelled to London to see the chief of prisons. Because Governor Number One governor had used the word *immature* to describe Dane's behaviour, it was classed as ageism. As a result, Dane was reinstated. This was much to the dissatisfaction of many staff at the prison. Once again, the bullying started. Dane ended up taking sickness leave because he experienced depression and stress. He never returned to the prison.

Just Me and an Inmate

I was walking through the prison grounds one morning, going from my department to another department. Each courtyard of the prison had gates to enter and exit through. On this morning, all of the inmates had just located to where they were supposed to be that day. Some would be working in the workshops, some would be in the education block, some would be in the kitchens, and some may have had appointments in the healthcare department or even outside of the prison.

I had just entered the healthcare courtyard and had locked the gate behind me. As I began to walk across the yard, I saw an inmate walking towards me. I quickly looked around, but I saw no staff or any other person. In a high-security prison, it is extremely rare for an inmate to be unaccompanied by an officer or two officers. This inmate was alone. I had just locked the gate behind me, which meant that it was just the two of us in the courtyard. As the inmate was approaching me, I could feel my heart racing. I began to sweat, but I couldn't let him see my fear. Then he asked me, "Will you let me into the healthcare unit, please, miss?" Now even though I had all the prison keys attached to my chain, I knew I couldn't do comply with his request. He may not have been allowed in the healthcare unit, as he may have been a threat to the staff or to other inmates in the unit. I was trying to weigh up the best thing to do, hoping and praying that I had been seen on camera. I could have pressed my alarm on my radio, but I didn't want to do that, as I used the alarm only as a last resort. Also, I didn't want the inmate thinking I was afraid.

I answered him by saying, "Why are you here alone? How have you got here?"

He replied, "I have been locked out. I am supposed to be in the healthcare unit, but when I got to the gate it was locked and there was no staff to escort me in. So can you just escort me in, please, miss?" I was still trying to work out the best thing to do without having the situation go pear-shaped. All the time, I was wishing someone would come to my aid. I told the inmate that I would use my radio to try to contact the officer from the wings who was responsible for him. At that point, he got agitated and said he needed to be in the unit straightaway. Then he came right into my personal space, very close to my face, and said, "Let me in." I thought he was going to attack me or strike me. As I looked over his shoulder, I saw two officers coming through the gate and entering the courtyard.

One of the officers read the situation very quickly and ran straight over to us. The other officer was very close behind. "What the hell is going on? Are you OK?" the first officer said, looking straight at me.

"Yes, I am fine, thanks," I answered. Then I explained exactly what had happened. The two officers were gobsmacked that an inmate was wandering around the prison alone. I also think they were more gobsmacked at the fact that it had just been me and the inmate for quite a few minutes in the courtyard and that control hadn't picked it up. The two officers took the inmate, asked again if I was OK, and went on their way.

Later that day, one of the two officers came to my department to see me and ask if I was OK. I told him I was fine and said that the inmate had been quite polite up until I was going to use my radio, at which point he became a little agitated. The officer then told me that there had been a major mistake that morning and somehow the inmate had ended up wandering about alone. He also told me that the inmate was serving a life sentence for raping and murdering three women. This inmate was a danger to women and was not allowed to be within ten metres of any female members of staff. I believe that someone must have been looking over me that day.

Missing Items

During the next few weeks, things were going fine in the works department. Everyone was getting on well, the work was going well, and we weren't having any problems. I got along with all my colleagues. Our friendships were getting stronger. I became quite close with Declan, another colleague of mine. Declan was a little older than I. He and I had a lot in common. We were both big supporters of our local rugby team. When my husband, our daughter, and I used to go to the home games on a Sunday, we would often meet up with Declan. Most of the conversations Declan and I had at work were about rugby. And he was one of the most hilarious blokes I had ever met. Some of the things he had done and gotten involved in were bizarre. For instance, for years he had been paying his neighbour's gas and electric bills and was totally unaware of it. He just presumed that gas and electric had risen extremely in price. He also helped people whom he thought were removal men carry a fridge, a television, and a microwave out of his neighbour's garden and then helped load them onto a wagon, not realising that the men were burglars! On another occasion, he had been shopping and bought his daughter a Leeds United shirt. He was really pleased with himself because he had gotten it at half price. For weeks he didn't see his daughter wearing it, so he asked her why. She explained to her dad that the first time she wore it, she was out with all her friends from college and thought that everyone was staring at her and laughing. Then someone had the decency to tell her that on the reverse of the shirt where it read *Leeds,* there was a misprint and the word was spelt with three *e*'s, *Leeeds*! This is why he had gotten it so cheap.

I believe that this was the same daughter who went travelling around Australia. She returned home unexpectedly, so she decided to surprise Declan. When he arrived home from work on this particular day, his daughter was, unbeknown to him, hiding in the boot of his other daughter's car. His other daughter asked him to help her get some stuff out of the boot. Declan told her to hang on a minute while he bobbed into the store across from his house. The other daughter went with him and was telling to hurry up, but he decided to get a trolley and do his weekly shopping. All this time, his other daughter was in the boot of the car. It was summer too, so one can imagine how hot it must have been for her. After Declan and his other daughter came out of the store, Declan decided to go into his house and put all the shopping away. By the time he went to his daughter's car and opened the boot, he found his other daughter in there, struggling to breathe. She had turned purple because of the heat. This wasn't the surprise she had been hoping to give him.

One of the most bizarre things Declan did was when he took his girlfriend to the A&E after she had gone over on her ankle. He was late coming into work that next morning. That was not like Declan. He was usually early, if anything. At work, he began telling us what had happened the night previous. His girlfriend had gone over on her ankle because of the height of the shoes she was wearing. So Declan had taken her up to the hospital. The two were in the waiting room when she was called through to see the doctor. She told Declan to wait for her in the waiting area and asked him to look after her a bag. He said that she was ages in there. He was unaware that a car accident had occurred and that the hospital staff were all dealing with the injured people from that incident. He said he was sitting there for almost two hours and his girlfriend still hadn't come back out. The next thing he knew, a name come up on the board: Declan Strongman. This was the same Christian name as Declan's, but a totally different surname from Declan's. No one went through to the doctors' area, so the name came back up on the board. For some reason, Declan got it into his head that they were calling for him. At this point in the story, my colleagues and I were stunned by the fact that he thought they were calling him. We asked him why he thought this. He replied, "Well, I had been waiting very long. I thought that they had maybe dealt with her but were struggling to help her walk and they needed a strong man to help, so when 'Declan Strongman' came up, I just got it in my head they wanted me to go help." We were in stitches! Then he said that when he went through, a nurse told him to go sit in a cubicle and said that someone would be along soon to see him. At this stage, he presumed that they must have taken his girlfriend for an X-ray or something, so he just sat on the bed and waited. In the meantime, his girlfriend had been dealt with. She had gone looking for Declan, but he was nowhere to be found. She looked all over the hospital. Having no bag because she had left it with Declan, she had no money. so she ended up walking all the way home with a strapped-up ankle.

Back at the hospital, a nurse eventually went into the cubicle where Declan was. He was sitting on the bed and holding his girlfriend's bright pink handbag. The nurse asked him if he was Declan Strongman. He said, "Well, no, I am not Declan Strongman, but I can explain where it has all gone wrong." He explained to the nurse what had happened, but she wasn't having any of it. I think it was the pink bag he was clutching that did him no favours. He ended up being escorted out of A&E by security. The guards held him most of the night until they eventually established what had happened. Hilarious.

Apart from his antics, Declan was a lovely chap. At work, he always did a great job and was always conscientious. One night, he was working overtime with some contactors who could only do this particular job after our working hours. When I was leaving that day, I did a handover with Declan. We checked all the tools, vehicle keys, etc., and then I signed everything over to Declan. The following morning once I arrived to work, someone handed me the keys. I noticed that a vehicle key was missing, the key to a dumper. It was obvious to me that on the previous evening, when Declan handed in all the keys, there was a key missing. This was a big security breach. I and the others in the works department all searched for this key down at the compound, but to no avail. When he found out about this, Declan was gutted. He couldn't understand what had happened, as he was sure that he had handed in all the keys. Once the security department got involved, the DST (dedicated search team) came down to do a check and a search, but still to no avail. The key never turned up. We in the works department had to create a better system set-up after this. Declan didn't have to face any disciplinary action for the missing key, which I was pleased about. The incident was over.

A few weeks later on a Friday, both Mitch and I were going on annual leave, so we had to choose one of the escorts to put in charge of the compound. No one wanted to do the job because on Fridays the DST would come to the works department and do a full check of the compound before the weekend. They would do tool checks and check to make sure that all the vehicles were locked and chained correctly. It never posed a problem to Mitch and me because we always made sure that everything was secure and checked, not just on a Friday, but on every day. But sometimes DST could be a little patronising, depending on which staff were on shift that particular day. So Bill offered to be in charge on the Friday when Mitch and I were both on leave. On that Thursday evening, we went through everything with Bill. He was satisfied with what we had told him to do. Bill was a great lad too. He was only a young lad. He had gone to school with my eldest daughter's partner, so that was something that Bill and I had in common. He also did some bizarre things. A massive Nottingham Forest Football Club fan, he used to go to a lot of the games. But he was always getting lost, getting on wrong trains and ending up in cities other than the ones where he intended to be. Even locally he would get lost. Now and then I would have a get-together at my house. At the house in which I lived at that time, Bruce and I had had our basement converted into a bar. My colleagues loved it. On one occasion, many co-workers and I were partying at my house and awaiting Bill. He had not been to my house before, but it was only about a mile from where he lived. I had given him the address. I thought it was impossible for him to get lost, but he did get lost. He had been away to a football match and had had quite a bit to drink. He had made it back to our town OK, but he couldn't find my house. He ended up going into the Chinese takeaway on the next street over from mine and asking a Chinese guy where I lived, saying that I was having a party. The Chinese guy had no idea what he was talking about or who I was. Bill was unable to use his phone, as he was non compos mentis, but the Chinese guy managed to find my number in the phone and ring me. I wondered who the hell it was when I answered. The takeaway worker explained that Bill was in his shop and couldn't find my house. I told him to tell Bill to come out of the shop, walk to the end of the street, turn left, and find the fifth house up. Bill decided to turn right instead of left, so he just carried on walking towards Leeds. Luckily, one of my colleagues had not been drinking. He was able to go find Bill and bring him back, ha.

Bill had a problem with his jaw. Sometimes it would just lock up and he would have to stretch his face a few times to unlock it. One morning when he was walking to work, his jaw locked. He was trying to unlock it, but he was struggling with the task. He approached a parked car and bent down to look in the driver's-side wing mirror. He began stretching his face and opening his mouth very wide while looking in the wing mirror. Little did he know that a woman was actually sitting in the car in the driver's side while he was doing this. She put the window down and asked him exactly what he was doing. He apologised, walked away, and was belly laughing all the way to work at what he had done.

So Bill was left in charge on this particular Friday. On that Friday evening, I wanted to make sure that everything had gone OK at work, so I sent Bill a text asking if all had been OK. He replied that everything had been fine, but that DST had not come down before the works department staff had left for the evening. This would happen occasionally and wasn't a problem, as the DST had keys to access all the tool sheds and could do checks without members of our staff being there. When we arrived at work on the next Monday morning, my co-workers and I were summoned into the meeting room in the estates department by our manager, Dick. Apparently, when DST went down on the Friday to do their checks, they found that the dumper had not been locked up and that the dumper key was on the seat of the dumper. Dick straightaway presumed it was down to Mitch and me, as Dick had not been at work on the previous Friday. Mitch and I explained that we had both been on annual leave and that Bill had been left in charge. We looked around and saw that Bill had not made it into work yet. He had probably gotten lost or was unlocking his jaw in someone's wing mirror. Anyway, we all had to endure a lecture from security and had to do a refresher training course on security issues. In addition, Mitch and I were informed that in future we would not be permitted to take annual leave on the same day, that there had to be one of us in charge at all times. No disciplinary action was taken against Bill. The incident was over.

Only about a week after this incident, Mitch and I were locking up one evening and we noticed that one of the huge locks that locked the big chains between vehicles was missing. We had a lot of these big locks, as there were quite a few vehicles at that time. We would chain all the vehicles together at the end of shift and then, on the following morning, unlock them all and take the big locks into the office until the end of shift. We knew we had to report the missing lock. If it got into the hands of an inmate, he would need a key and a chain – things he would not be able to access – to use it. Still, the lock could be used as a weapon. So Mitch and I reported the missing lock through the correct channels. A search began. The lock was never found, so we had to have the chub locks replaced with new ones. This way, there were different keys, just in case the lock had made it into the wrong hands. Dick blamed me, Mitch, and Drew for the missing lock.

The locks had never been put down on a tool inventory in all the time Mitch and I had been in the works department. When we took over the compound, we just followed suit and did the same procedure that Drew had done. After this event with the lock, however, Mitch and I began putting the locks and chains on the tool inventory. But it was a mystery where the lock had gone. DST presumed that a contractor had picked it up mistakenly and then taken it out of the prison. I was unsure about that.

A few weeks later, I was in Dick's office having my SPDR (staff progress and development report). Dick was rummaging through his drawer and looking for a red pen. He was removing things from the drawer and placing them on his desk. The next item he placed on his desk was a chub lock! I looked at him and asked, "Dick, is that the missing lock?"

He became all flustered. Coughing and shuffling about, he replied, "Yes." I asked him why the hell it was in his drawer. He said that he had gone down to the compound one day to borrow a lock in order to lock up some ladders in the estates department. Mitch and I were both busy with something, so he just took the lock off our desk. He then let a contractor use it that day up at the estates. At the end of shift, instead of bringing the lock back, Dick put it in his drawer and then totally forgot about it. He was my manager, but I still went mad at him. I told him that Mitch, Drew, and I had all taken the blame from him. I mentioned all the hassle the incident had caused with security and with our having to have all new locks and so forth. He apologised to me but said he couldn't come clean now, as it had gone too far. He said he was going to try sneak the lock out of the prison, but he was unsure how to do it, as he may be subjected an exit search when leaving the prison. So he said he would try to put the lock into a skip that was leaving the prison. I told him that I hadn't heard what he had said. I don't know if he ever got rid of that lock. He never mentioned it after that. The lesson here is that if you are an OSG and something goes wrong or something goes missing, then you have to be retrained or attend refresher courses. If you are a manager, then you can do what you want, apparently.

Brothers

I have seven brothers in total. They are all older than I and, therefore, they have always looked out for me. I am very close to all of my brothers. I love them all dearly.

Willie bought a place in Spain a few years ago. It was an old farm up in the mountains. He renovated it and made it beautiful. My brother Colin, who is just a little younger than Willie, moved out to Spain not long after Willie had bought his place over there. Colin originally went over to recuperate after having a heart scare. He intended to stay for only a few weeks. He never came home to live, only the odd time to visit the family. He managed to get some work in Spain. He also got himself a nice little place to live. In other words, Colin was sorted. Willie used the place he had bought in Spain for holidays with his wife and their children. He spent most of his time in England.

My husband and I have a place on the east coast. We spend most of our weekends there. When I joined the Prison Service and Bruce and I had an extra wage coming in, we decided to buy this little place. We were thinking about our future, as we believe that property is a better investment than a pension is. We were fortunate enough at that time to be able to spend most weekends on the east coast. My shifts in the works department were Monday to Friday, so Bruce and I could head over to our second place on a Friday evening after work, spend the weekend there, and return home on a Sunday afternoon.

It was Sunday, 20 September 2009. I had just returned home from the coast and was checking my house phone to see if I had any messages. I was taken aback when I heard a message from a solicitor telling me that my brother Colin had been arrested and was being held at Dewsbury Police Station. I couldn't get my head around it, as I had thought Colin was in Spain. The solicitor had left a number for me to call him, so this I did. Once I called, the solicitor told me that Colin had been arrested just past Dartford Tunnel and that the police had brought him to Yorkshire; hence, he was been held at Dewsbury Police Station. The solicitor said that Colin had been arrested on suspicion of having drugs in a caravan which he was bringing back to England from Spain. I could not quite believe this, as Colin had never been in trouble in his life. Then within minutes, I got a call from my mum saying that Willie had been arrested and was being held at Selby Police Station. Bruce and I could not work out what had happened with both lads being arrested but being held at different police stations. It turned out that Colin was returning to England to make a surprise visit to his son Dave, who was going to turn twenty-one in the next day or so. Colin had been towing a touring caravan from Spain back to England and was supposed to be dropping this caravan off somewhere in Yorkshire. We weren't expecting Colin home. He had wanted to surprise us all, most of all his son.

The police at both stations would not inform me of anything regarding the arrests. All they told me was that both of my brothers would be appearing in court the following morning. I was deeply shocked. Colin had never encountered any trouble before, so all sorts of things were going through my mind about the state he must have been in. I contacted his son Dave, who was totally unaware of what was going on. I asked him if he had any idea that his dad intended to come home. Dave said that he wasn't positive his dad was coming home, but he did have an inkling that he may turn up for his twenty-first birthday.

I realised that it was my duty to report to my superiors at the prison that my brothers had been arrested. First thing Monday morning, once I arrived at the prison, I went straight to my line manager, Dick, and informed him that my two brothers had been arrested. At that point, I could not tell him much more, as I was waiting to learn what happened in court. Dick informed me that I had to go report it immediately to the security department. The security department is all open plan. As soon as I entered, all eyes were on me. I asked if I could speak to the principal officer in private. The principal officer on duty that particular morning was the same principal officer who had pulled me out of training the previous year. "Great," I thought, "this is all I need." After I informed her of my brothers' arrests, she was quite sympathetic towards me. She could clearly see that I was very upset about the whole thing and told me not to worry about it too much. She made notes of my brothers' names and the police stations where they were being held. She then told me that as soon as I knew the outcome from court, I had to inform security immediately.

I returned to my duties. After lunchtime, I telephoned my husband to see if there was any news. He told me that my brothers had been charged with importing Class A drugs and that they had been remanded to prison. He was unaware of which prison or prisons they had been sent to. I could not comprehend was happening. I was absolutely gutted and felt sick in the bottom of my stomach. I feared for Colin, as he had never been in trouble. He was forty-seven at the time, and during his forty-seven years he had never put a foot wrong. I could not imagine how he must have been feeling at that time. Willie would be more aware of the situation, as he had served time in his younger years. My only hope at the time was that the two were together. I consoled myself by thinking that Willie could take care of Colin. My worst fear was that they had been separated and that Colin was alone. I was unsure at that time which prison they had been sent to. I believe that the prison protocol is as follows: If a staff member's sibling or family member is in the same prison as the staff member, then the staff member can choose whether the sibling moves to a different prisons or the staff member herself moves to a different prison. (Keep in mind though, that a friend of mine who, at that time, worked at another local prison informed me that a male nurse who worked in the healthcare department at that prison had a brother who was serving time in that same prison.) The prison where I worked had a remand centre. I feared that my brothers may have been sent there.

I went straight back to the security department to inform them. I saw the same principal officer. She asked me to which prison my brothers had been remanded. I told her I did not know. She told me to report back to her as soon as I found out.

I returned home that evening and awaited a call from Colin, as I knew I would be the first person he would contact. At 7 p.m., my phone rang. When I answered, I heard Colin's voice on the other end. He was in a terrible state; he was a broken man. He told me that he and Willie had been taken to the other local prison, the one to which I had originally applied, and were now in the reception area awaiting a cell. Willie was on another telephone to his wife, so I didn't get to speak to him that night. Colin was absolutely broken. I could hear it in his voice. He did say that he was relieved that he and Willie had not been separated. I told Colin to keep his chin up and said that I would visit him as soon as I could.

The following morning, I went straight to security to give them an update and to ask the requirements for applying for visits. I saw the same principal officer again, only this time she did not seem quite as sympathetic. She did tell me, however, that people can't be made to answer for what their family members do. She also told me that her own cousin was doing time for the next few years for a similar offence. She then informed me, regarding visitations, that she would look into the matter, but I would have to wait until visits had been passed. She told me not to book any visits until I heard from her.

Earlier that week, Colin's son Dave had visited his dad. Willie was getting regular visits from his wife and children. Colin was awaiting some money being sent in to him for his phone calls and other things. He had told his son that he was desperate for me to visit him as, other than his son, he had only me to visit him. Colin had been divorced for quite some years and didn't have a partner. During that week, I received no calls from security to say that my visits had been passed. On 28 September, Colin phoned me and pleaded with me to visit him. I had to explain to him that I was awaiting approval for my visits and that I couldn't visit either him or Willie until I had gotten permission. The following day, I went back to security and told the principal officer that my brother was desperate. I needed to know how long I would have to wait before my visits were approved. The PO said to me, "Oh, didn't I tell you last week that you have to put it in writing to Governor Number One to request visits?" I was furious because, no, she hadn't told me that I had to put it in writing to the governor. Now a full week had passed. I was back to square one. I wrote immediately that day, 29 September, to the governor and requested my visits. I also requested permission to send money in to Colin.

That week, both of my brothers were moved from the prison they were in to another prison, one which was privately run. Every night, both brothers contacted me to see if I had gotten my visits passed. I had to keep telling them the same old thing. Days passed by. I still had not been contacted by security. I continued to go up to the security department, but to no avail. The PO just kept telling me the same thing: "Not yet." Colin was not getting many visits, only occasional ones from his son, as it was quite difficult for Dave with his work commitments and with travelling to the prison. It was totally unfair that the prison where I worked was taking so long to get back to me. I could have understood it if my brothers had been remanded for murder or another very serious crime. Remember that they were not convicted; they were on remand. As the weeks passed, both my brothers and I were desperate to have visits.

On 5 November while I was walking through the prison grounds, I saw the governor from security. I approached him and asked if my visits had been passed. He said, "Oh yes. Just go visit your brothers. It's absolutely fine." I asked him if this was the word from Governor Number One. He replied that it was. He seemed very casual in the way that he told me this, as if he didn't have to think about it, as if he had said it off the top of his head. Either way, I was elated by the fact I could go visit my brothers. Later that day, I got a call on my radio asking me if I would attend the security department before the end of my shift. I went up just after my shift had finished. I saw the principal officer again. She informed me that I had to inform security before each visit and also after each visit. I had to make notes of the conversations I had on each visit, and I had to log every telephone call that my brothers made to me. I thought this a bit bizarre, having to make notes of our conversations, but I was prepared to go through anything in order to have my visits.

The PO then dropped a right bombshell. She told me I could visit only Colin, and not Willie. I asked her why. She said, "Willie is the instigator and is high profile. You must not visit him."

Stunned, I asked her, "What about innocent until proved guilty?" She just glared at me. I said, "My brothers are on remand. They have not been sentenced. They have not been on trial. This is totally unfair what you are saying to me."

She looked at me with a promising look and said, "Like I said, you may visit Colin, but not Willie. If you do visit Willie, you will lose your job." I walked out of the prison that day with mixed feelings. I was happy, very happy that my visits had been passed, yet I felt very deflated that I couldn't visit Willie. It just didn't seem fair.

As soon as I arrived home that evening, I contacted the prison where my brothers were being held. I booked a visit for Colin. Not long after that, my brothers phoned me. Colin was the first on to call. Once I gave him the good news, he was overwhelmed. Then he put Willie on the phone. I had to tell Willie that I could not visit him. He was gutted. When I came off the phone, I was heartbroken over the fact that I had to tell my brother, whom I love very much, that I wasn't allowed to visit him. My husband comforted me and told me that it wouldn't be long before my brothers were released – and then I could see Willie again. The thing that really niggled me was that my manager, Dick, had a son who was in care, in a secure unit, for committing sexual offences against his own sibling. Dick could visit his son every Tuesday and probably on weekends too. My brother was on remand, had not been tried, and had not been sentenced, but I had the privilege to visit him taken from me. That is absurd. There was one rule for the OSG and one rule for the manager. Where's the fairness there?

When I visited Colin, he was overwhelmed when he saw me. I had been waiting for this day. Once it arrived, I found that my instincts were correct. Previous to my visit, I was aware that I would know straightaway whether my brothers were innocent or guilty just from my first visit with Colin. What he told me that day what had happened, it confirmed my suspicion that everything had been a set-up. The police and the courts obviously thought differently, and so did many others, but I knew that Colin was telling me the truth. He would have told me the truth either way, whether he and Willie were innocent or guilty.

Every single night, both of my brothers rang me. It was always around the same time, between 5.40 p.m. and 6.15 p.m., just after they had had tea. If ever I was running late or had been late getting out of work, I tried my hardest to get home so I didn't miss their calls. I hated it if I did miss them. As instructed, I logged each phone call, writing down the date, the time, and how long we were on the phone. Prior to each visit, I had to inform security. After each visit, I had to inform security and also tell them about the conversations I had had. I think they were taking the urine out of me, to be honest, because they would ask me how many drinks and bars of chocolates I bought Colin during our visit. It was unbelievable. Each time I visited Colin, he was subjected to a strip search before returning to his cell. Also, I began noticing at work that I was being searched more and more upon leaving the prison. One would only be subjected to an exit search now and then. Sometimes one could go weeks and weeks without having an exit search. But, like I said, my exit searches were occurring more and more often. It got to the stage where I was being searched two or three times a week. Then it was almost every day. I reached a point where, upon leaving the prison, I simply walked back towards the search area because I knew what was coming. I really don't know what the higher-ups thought I would be trying to take out of the prison.

Willie and Colin had gotten themselves nice little jobs in the kitchens at their prison. They weren't housed on the main wings; instead, they had been put on a wing where just the kitchen staff was housed. All of the officers on that wing were good people, apparently. When Willie told them that I wasn't allowed to visit him, they found it astonishing and said that the prison security had no right to deny me. Willie told them that I was afraid of losing my job and, therefore, didn't want to risk anything by booking a visit. The officers at my brother's prison felt sorry for Willie and me. They said that they found it very unfair that I had two brothers who were on remand in the same prison and who were charged with the same crime, yet I could visit only one of them. So what they did was this: they told Willie to get his wife to book a visit for the same time when I booked a visit to see Colin. This we did. When I and Willie's wife were visiting Colin and Willie in prison, we found that the officers had put our tables next to each other. It was lovely and perfect. I never booked a visit to see Willie, but each time I visited Colin I got to see Willie. And when I was leaving the visit, I could give Willie a hug. The officers were aware that he was my brother and that I wasn't just hugging random inmates. Ha.

That Christmas was the worst. I had booked a visit for Christmas Eve. So had Willie's wife. We had a lunchtime visit. That morning when I got up, it was thick with snow. Cars were slipping and sliding on the road outside, and vehicles were getting stuck. Public transport had stopped. It was a blizzard. I thought, "Oh my days, how am I going to get to the prison in this terrible weather?" Then I said to myself, "It's Christmas Eve. I have to see my brothers if I have to walk twenty miles. I have to see my brothers." So my husband, our youngest daughter, and I set off about two hours early. I didn't want to miss the visit. I was aware that if we arrived late, the guards wouldn't let us through. Then I would have a vision in my head of my brothers awaiting a visit and us not turning up. I couldn't have lived with myself if that happened.

Bruce and I struggled in the bad weather, but we arrived at the prison with about fifteen minutes to spare. The visiting area was very quiet. It was obvious that a lot of families and other loved ones had not made it through the snow. Willie's wife had also arrived safely, which pleased me, as I wouldn't have seen Willie had she not turned up. My brothers were elated when they walked into the visiting area. I believe their thoughts were that we wouldn't get there. It was a quiet visit, especially when it came to the end and we had to say goodbye. Colin handled it quite well, considering that he had never been in prison, let alone locked up at Christmastime. Willie, on the other hand, was heartbroken. It tore me apart to see Willie's youngest boy clinging to his father's legs and asking why his dad wasn't going to be at home when Father Christmas came. I cried all the way home in the car.

The following day, I lived Willie and Colin's day for them. I know the prison routine, so every day I could picture what they would be doing. But Christmas Day was worse. My colleague Declan had come to my and Bruce's house for Christmas dinner. Just as we sat down for dinner and to listen to the Queen's speech, the phone rang. It was my brothers. I had the biggest lump in my throat one could imagine having. I held it together on the phone, but as soon as I came off I cried. I felt stupid for crying in front of Declan.

Christmas went as quickly as it had come. Then New Year's Eve arrived. Bruce, I, and our children went to our place at the coast and had a quiet holiday. I was glad when it was all over, to be honest.

After the New Year, I returned to work unaware that my brothers' arrests, charges, and remands had been posted on the Internet. I began to endure sarcastic comments from a lot of the officers at work, even officers I didn't know. One officer walked past me and said, "Oh, you're the one that's got brothers inside looking at a twelve-year stretch, aren't you?" I just ignored him. Obviously bored with his own sad life, he had a go at me.

Then I got it a lot. Officers made remarks when they walked past me. They made remarks in the search area in the morning, saying things like, "Watch her. She's probably got two kilos of sniff in her prison bag" and "Here, look, it's the coke importers' sister. Surprised you still got your job, darling." I heard comment after comment with great frequency. And I knew that if I said anything to anyone, I would get nowhere and it would make things worse for me in the prison, so I just kept my mouth shut and ignored people the best I could.

Even my own governor from the works department called me in to his office one day, saying he wanted a chat. When I walked in, I saw that he had his computer on. He said, "Here, look, a bloke was just convicted of the same crime as your brothers. Fifteen years he got."

I asked, "Is that what you wanted me for?"

He said, "Well, we have to be realistic, Liz. Your brothers are going away for a hell of a long time. What are you going to do then?"

I said, "Well, with all due respect, Mr P, firstly, how do we know they are going away? They have not been tried yet. And secondly, what do you mean, what am I going to do then? What do you mean?"

He replied, "Well, if they get sentenced, you won't be able to visit as often as you do now. Would you be able to take the stick you would get if they did go down for a long time?"

I hit straight back and said, "I am getting stick now. They haven't been found guilty, so nothing will change there. I am being realistic, like you so eloquently said, and I believe my brothers to be innocent."

Mr P coughed and spat out a mouthful of coffee. "We are talking about Willie here, for God's sake." I asked him if I was free to leave. He said I was. When I left his office, I was fuming. I, unlike many staff who said he was arrogant and self-righteous, always liked Mr P. I always got along with him, but this day I also thought he was arrogant and self-righteous.

February 2010 approached. Colin's solicitor was preparing a bail application for him. Until his trial, Colin obviously could not return to Spain, where he lived, so he had to be bailed in England. His solicitor contacted me and informed me that Colin wanted to be bailed to my address. At work, I went to see someone in the security department. I had a feeling prior to my asking for permission to house Colin that it would be an uphill struggle. Look how long it took me to get my visits passed and at the hassle I experienced when I wanted to visit Willie. It was a straight not-a-cat-in-hell's chance. I had more prospects of becoming pope. After security denied my request, I had to tell Colin and his solicitor that it was a no go. On 17 March 2010, Colin was granted bail. He was to be bailed to his son Dave's address. He was on tag from 7 p.m. to 7 a.m. and had to sign bail each week. I informed security that he had gotten bail. They told me that I could visit him at his bail address, but that I could not have him visit me at my home address. One week later, Willie was granted bail. He was to be bailed to his home address. He was on twenty-four-hour tag. Once again, I informed security. They told me the same, that I could visit Willie at his bail address. They couldn't really tell me that Willie couldn't visit me, as he was on twenty-four-hour tag. So both lads were out. Willie didn't have much freedom, but he was out and awaiting trial. I spent a lot of my spare time visiting both brothers at their bail addresses. It was difficult, as they lived about forty miles apart, but it was much better than visiting them in prison.

My brothers were to have separate trials. I don't know why this was. Willie said it would be better if Colin was on trial first. He also mentioned that it was imperative they have separate trial dates. Colin's trial was set for July 2010 at Leeds Crown Court. Prior to this, I asked someone in the security department if I could attend the trial, just purely to support my brother and his son Dave. The answer was a straight no. They said it was a conflict of interest and also that I would be bringing the prison into disrepute. When the trial date came, security told me not to even take annual leave. They said they would have some prison official in attendance at the court in case I decided to turn up. That seemed a little extreme to me, but there you go.

When Colin's trial started, I went in to work as normal, but I was a dithering wreck. I was phoning home, but to no avail. My colleagues were telling me that the trial would probably last all week anyway and not to get myself too worked up.

I always used to leave my mobile phone in my car when I was at work. I could have taken it with me and put it in a locker outside the prison, but I feared leaving it in my bag and taking it in. If one had a phone in one's possession when going through the search area, then there was hell on. That person would find herself up in front of the governor. The phone would be sent away to be analysed. Plus, given the treatment I had received at the prison, I think that if ever I had been caught in possession of my phone, I would have been hung, drawn, and quartered. So the first day of Colin's trial, I left the prison after my shift, got in my car, and checked my phone. I had seven text messages, from my two eldest daughters; my husband; Dave; Dave's girlfriend; my mum; and Willie. All the messages read the same: NOT GUILTY. I sat and cried. I sat for about ten minutes before I could take control of myself. I felt sheer relief. I was very pleased for Colin, happy about the fact that he could get on with his life. I was very pleased for myself too, as I realised that things could only get better for me at work.

That night, my family celebrated. We laughed and we cried and we hugged. It was wonderful. I had my brother back.

The following day, I went to work. My first port of call was security. I saw the principal officer. She said, "Well, that's one down and one to go. And I don't think Willie will be as lucky as Colin."

I said, "I don't believe it was down to luck. I believe it was down to innocence, and so did the jury." I left security. As I walked down to the works department, I wasn't at all bothered about what the principal officer had said to me. She could have said anything at all. My brother was innocent, and that was all that mattered to me.

Colin decided to stay in England for a while. He had had a bad time over the past ten months, going to prison, being out on bail, facing trial, etc., so Bruce and I let him move into our place at the coast. Within a month, he had gotten himself a nice little flat in the town centre, not far from our place. He also got himself a nice little job down at the harbour. Happy days.

Willie's trial was yet to come.

Adam and Eve

When I first met Adam and Eve, I was very unsure about the both of them. I first met them in 2008, which was when I joined the Prison Service and was placed at the works department. I thought they didn't like me to begin with, as they didn't speak a word to me for the first week or so. Adam, a little intimidating, was an overweight, loud-mouthed Geordie. Wherever I was in the prison, I could hear Adam shouting and bawling, mostly about his football team, Sunderland. I believe a few people at the prison weren't big lovers of Adam, but once I got to know him, I actually liked him. I think Eve didn't speak much to me in the beginning because before I joined the team, she was the only female. There were around seventeen or eighteen people in the team at the beginning. I believe that Eve, being the only female at the time, felt a little threatened by another female joining the team. But as time went on, she and I became good friends. Even though we became good friends, something in the back of my mind told me that she just wasn't ringing true.

I could never comprehend how Adam and Eve could spend so much time together. They were married, so they lived together. Also, they worked together. Not only were they on the same shift in the same department but also they always partnered each other. If the rota put them with different partners for a week, then they would ignore the rota and just work together. As I got to know them both, I realised that was Eve's doing. She was the one who didn't want Adam partnering up with anyone else, especially with me. Our manager at the time, Mr H, completely changed the whole working pattern. Whomever one was partnered with on the rota was the person with whom one worked. Adam didn't really mind which person he worked with. When Adam and I were partnered, Eve's mood would change. I liked Adam as a friend and as a work colleague, and that was it. I believe it was the same for him. I had some really nice conversations with Adam, just as I did with Eve. We all became friends and had some good times, at work, on nights out, and during the weekend away we all had in Sunderland. My husband even set Eve's son on as an apprentice. Unfortunately, after a while, Bruce had to let him go, as the young lad just wasn't cut out to be a heating engineer.

During the bad time I was having when my brothers were arrested and then sent to prison, Eve was a really good friend to me. She listened to me when I wanted to get things off my chest. She used to ring or text me every night to see if my brothers had rung me and to ask how I was. Sometimes she would cry when I told her how hard the visits were, especially the Christmas visit. She was chuffed to bits when Colin received the verdict of not guilty. She was hoping for the best for Willie too. She was very understanding. I knew I could talk to her.

But it was ironic, really, because Eve was also having a bad time with her own brother. He was an alcoholic and had lots of medical problems. He was in and out of hospital often. It was a very worrying time for Eve. But I was there for her. And it wasn't just me listening to her. I felt like I had come to know her brother even though I had never met him. I was genuinely concerned for him and for Eve too. If Eve didn't text me on a night, I would text her to see how things were with her brother. Sometimes she would come into work and would cry and cry for her brother. Basically, she was watching him slowly die. He had to stop the drinking, but he couldn't. His mind would go and he would end up getting sectioned. He would be on the mend for a while, but Eve knew that he would go back to the drinking. And she was right, as he always did. I felt very sorry for her. I don't think that Adam always showed Eve the compassion she wanted. I think that sometimes Adam thought that Eve's brother just wouldn't help himself, so why should anyone else? But alcoholism is an illness. It takes a lot of courage for a person to put it right.

I know things weren't always good between Adam and Eve. They both talked to me about things but asked me not to tell the other one. This put me in a predicament, as they were both my friends. Sometimes I wished they would not tell me anything. Eve had a bit of a thing for my brother Alan. Nothing ever came of it because my brother wouldn't get involved, given that Eve was married. Alan said that he had seen the size of Adam and wouldn't fancy taking him on.

When I became good friends with Mitch, Eve didn't really like it. She liked it even less when Mitch and I were put in charge, even though it was she and Adam who had wanted Drew out. In September 2010, Adam, for some reason, had it in for Mitch. We at work didn't know why, but he started on Mitch the same way he had started on Drew – and Kerry and Dane. He began to intimidate, humiliate, and bully Mitch. It wasn't nice to see, as Mitch and I were really good friends. I was also friends, of course, with Adam and Eve, but Mitch was much more of a friend to me. It began with Adam asking Mitch something. If Mitch didn't answer straightaway, then Adam would get right up close into Mitch's face and shout, "Just answer the fucking question." Then he would repeat, "Just answer the fucking question." He was plainly and clearly intimidating Mitch. This went on for a while, and it was getting Mitch down. I had seen this all before with Kerry, with Drew, and with Dane. Now it was Mitch's turn.

Eve would just laugh when Adam was humiliating Mitch. I hated it. I asked Adam on the quiet if he would stop doing what he was doing to Mitch. Normally, Adam would have just shouted and bawled if anyone asked him to do something he didn't want to do, but with me he just ignored my question. Adam continued at Mitch. On one occasion, Adam made a comment to Mitch about me. Mitch never told me exactly what Adam had said because he said he had too much respect for me to repeat the filth that had come out of Adam's mouth. Mitch did tell me that it was along the lines of "Just admit it, Mitch. You want to shag Liz all over this office, don't you?" Mitch said that Adam was saying really crude things about what he thought Mitch wanted to do to me. He didn't want to repeat the exact, explicit words that Adam had used, out of respect for me. Mitch was more upset because of the good friendship that he and I had and because of the fact that he was married. He hated the fact that Adam said such things. Mitch was extremely happily married and still is now, and that's what upset him more than anything, that someone would think unsavoury things about him.

I told Mitch not to worry about it and to try to ignore Adam. But that was easier said than done, because Adam got worse and worse towards Mitch. The other lads in our team would just laugh when Adam was on at Mitch. For some reason, they seemed to look up to Adam. I think it was because he was loud and large. Drew didn't find Adam's behaviour amusing, as he had been on the receiving end of

Adam's bullying before. I didn't find it amusing, as I had also endured bullying – not from Adam though. Plus, Mitch was a very good friend to me, and even if he weren't, I can't tolerate bullying. But again, it is very difficult in the prison. If you can't sort something out yourself, then you have no chance. So this is what Mitch did: he got Adam alone and had a word with him. He told Adam that he didn't appreciate the way he spoke to him and the way he tried to intimidate and humiliate him. He said he didn't like the things he had said about me and then asked him politely to lay off. Mitch told me that Adam's demeanour was quite calm and that he reacted by apologising and saying that it wouldn't happen again. That lasted for about two and a half hours before Adam was back to his usual self, constantly getting at Mitch.

It was 28 October 2010. Mitch couldn't take it any longer. He had reached the point that both Dane and I had reached in the past, not wanting to come in to work and worrying at home about the next day's work. Mitch had had enough. He said he was going up to see Dick and was going to have a quiet word informally. He wanted to see what Dick would come up with so he didn't have to make a formal complaint. Mitch asked me if I would go up with him to provide moral support. I said, "Of course I will." We went to the canteen at lunchtime like we did many a day, but on the way, we went up to the estates department to see Dick. Unfortunately, Dick was on leave that day (it was probably a Tuesday). So Mitch asked if he could speak to another line manager or the manager who was covering for Dick that day. The line manager that day was Chris, so Mitch and I went into Chris's office. Mitch began to tell Chris what had been going on. Mitch said he knew it would be difficult for Chris to keep the matter quiet, but he asked if he would keep it quiet for the moment, as we all knew the consequences when something like this came out. Chris reassured Mitch and said he was fully aware of what Adam was like. Something had to come to a head, Chris said. There were many complaints against Adam, but nothing ever seemed to be done about the problem. Chris told Mitch to leave the matter with him, saying that he would speak to Dick once he returned, after which point he would get back to Mitch.

That day at the end of our shift, my colleagues and I headed up to the estates department to hand in our radios and the works keys we had. As we were handing them in and signing out, Chris called a staff meeting straightaway. He said he wanted everyone to appear in the meeting room before we left the prison. Mitch and I looked at each other. There was nothing we could do at that stage. The other escorts were all talking amongst themselves, wondering why there was to be a meeting at that time of the day. As we were all heading into the meeting room, Chris put his hand in front of Mitch and said, "Not you, Mitch." Then he put his hand in front of me and said, "Not you either, Liz." He led all the escorts into the meeting room and told Mitch and me to go sit in the office next door. So he had called a staff meeting but had omitted Mitch and me from the meeting. We couldn't believe it, as Mitch had purposely asked Chris to keep the complaint quiet for the moment.

Mitch and I had our ears to the wall and could hear everything that was said. Craig said that a complaint had been made regarding bullying and that the bullying had to stop. If it didn't, then the matter would be taken farther, he said. We could hear Adam asking very loudly who had made the complaint. Chris said that he had nothing else to say other than that the bullying must stop now. Obviously, the fourteen other members of staff presumed that it was I and Mitch who had made the complaint, hence our absence from the meeting.

We heard Chris leave the office and then leave the building. Then we heard all the others leaving the office. They were talking about the impromptu meeting. We heard Adam say very loudly, "Well, we know who's been up here grassing, don't we?"

Eve replied, "Yeah, those two bastards."

Our fourteen co-workers left the building. Mitch and I were left completely gobsmacked. All Mitch could do was apologise to me, as he knew that he was the one who had gone to management about Adam and that I had just accompanied him in order to give him moral support, but now it looked like I was the one who had made the complaint. I told Mitch not to worry about it, that it was very unprofessional what Chris had done and that I was getting used to grief in that prison anyway. Mitch and I said goodnight, got in our cars, and went home. My husband couldn't believe what Chris had done and was upset because the latter had probably now put me in a difficult situation at work. I told my husband that I would go see Dick about it, as I knew I was to expect grief at work.

The following morning, Mitch and I met in the car park. We were dreading going into the prison. We were correct in our assumptions, as hardly anyone spoke to us when we arrived. Adam and Eve totally blanked us, as did most of the other staff in our team. Drew and Kieran were the only ones who spoke to us. Kieran was always OK with me. I knew him from my local village. In fact, I had known him for quite a few years before I joined the Prison Service.

During that day, both Mitch and I tried to explain to our colleagues what had happened the day previous. Mitch was totally honest and said that he was the one who had gone to talk to Chris. He mentioned that I had only gone to support him, but this didn't help me. Our co-workers gave us the silent treatment. Eve always used to sit at the side of my desk in the office so we could talk to each other, but on this day she had moved herself to the very bottom of the office. It was very uncomfortable that day at work because even Kelvin, with whom I had initially done my training, blanked me. This upset me considerably, as Kelvin and I got on very well. When I tried to explain to Kelvin and my other colleagues what had happened, I found that they didn't want to know.

After our shift, Mitch and I went to see Dick. We told him exactly what Chris had done and how he had dealt with the situation. Dick said he would have to do something about that because, yes, it was totally unprofessional and Chris had put us, me more than Mitch, in a very bad situation.

Over the next week or so, things got much worse at work. Eve's behaviour towards me was the worst. As I was in charge at that time, all the communication through the works department radios was done by me. When I called Eve for something, she would not respond through her radio. On these radios, all of the managers of the works department could hear what was said, so management were fully aware that Eve wasn't responding to me via her radio. This was a major security issue, as it was essential for prison workers to contact each other through the radio in order to make sure that security protocol was adhered to and that staff members were safe. However, management did nothing about Eve's refusal to respond to me through the radio. Eve then persuaded other members of staff to totally blank both me and Mitch. The funny thing was that our colleagues would speak to us when Adam and Eve weren't there, but they blanked us as soon as the couple were present. Drew and Kieran always spoke to Mitch and me whether Adam and Eve were there or not.

On 12 November 2010, I spoke to Dick unofficially about Adam and Eve. He actually asked me how things were going down at the compound, as he and other managers had noticed that things weren't right. He mentioned Eve's failure to respond over the radio, the terrible atmosphere between staff, and so forth. I asked him what he expected after what Chris had done. Dick said that he would call me to his office on the following Monday, at which time he would try to sort things out. He said that something had to be done regarding Adam, as too many complaints had been made against him. Now that Mitch had made a complaint, something had to be done. Neither Mitch nor I was called to Dick's office on that Monday, but Adam was.

Adam was removed from our department and was put on the yard party, working with the binmen. He was informed that he could not return to the works department and could not have any contact with Mitch. This happened around lunchtime. Well, one can imagine the reaction from Eve when she found out that Adam had been removed. She was furious. However would she cope with not having her husband by her side 24/7? She spoke individually to all the staff and asked them to accompany her to see Dick and protest against Adam's being moved. I am unsure how many of the staff actually backed her up and accompanied her to see Dick.

Drew was my and Mitch's informer. He would listen to and pick up what Eve was saying to the other staff, and then he would come and report to us. Drew wasn't bothered about doing this, as he disliked both Adam and Eve. Kieran also told me and Mitch things that Eve was trying to do. I don't think that Kieran was a big lover of Adam, but I do know that he disliked Eve. So at least Mitch and I had two members of our team who were still speaking to us.

Soon, Eve began to turn the contractors against both Mitch and me. This was very difficult for her, seeing as Mitch and I were in charge of the compound. When Eve needed a key signed out or if she needed any tools marked off the inventory, she would ask someone else to do it for her so that she didn't have to acknowledge me. I thought this was very childish on her part, very school-playground style and, more than anything, very unprofessional. Saying that, even when Eve and I were friends, I thought she was very unprofessional and sometimes ignorant. She would never hold a gate for another member of staff. She would often blank members of staff when they spoke to her. I think the most unprofessional thing about her though was how she spoke about the inmates. If she was awaiting a move acknowledgement over the radio when she wanted to take contractors to a certain place in the prison, and if she was told to hold her move because there were inmates moving, she would say to the contractors, "We can't move yet. There's freak movement." Or she would say, "We can't move till they have got the fucking weirdo paedophiles out of the way." Sometimes she would say these things in front of officials from the home office. They would look at her in disgust. I am very surprised she never got reported. I am also surprised that her own safety was never compromised, as she would call out the inmates as she walked past them. It is never a prison worker's job to pass judgement on what the inmates had done to end up in prison. Neither is it a prison worker's job to be judge or jury. The inmates had obviously been found guilty and had been sentenced. It is a prison worker's job to protect the public and keep the inmates inside the prison. Sometimes I wondered why Eve worked at the prison. She never wanted to work on the wings because of the inmates. She wished every inmate dead. Wouldn't she have been out of a job if they were all dead?

I found it increasingly difficult to be at work. All I wanted to do was do my job correctly, but Eve was hindering me. She breached security protocol, put not only staff but also contractors at risk, and basically made my job a whole lot harder than it should have been. The thing that wound me the most was the fact that since all of the works managers could hear everything over our radios, it must have been clear to them that Eve was making obstructions and avoiding security protocol just so she didn't have to converse with me. It was bizarre that none of the managers did anything about this problem.

I had encountered enough. On 17 November, I went to see Dick in the estates department. Prior to this, I had spoken with Mitch and had told him that since he had made the complaint against Adam and it was misconstrued, most of the staff had it in for me, so I had nothing to lose by going to see Dick. I told Dick everything. Most importantly, I asked if he and the other managers could hear what Eve had been doing over the works radios. He replied, "Well, yes, I have heard, but I presumed it would work itself out." I told him about the bad atmosphere in the works department. I said that my job wasn't getting done properly and that Eve was putting the contactors and everyone in the works department in danger. I reminded him that this had started because Chris had omitted me and Mitch from that staff meeting. Dick told me that he was submitting what I said as an official complaint and that he would begin to look into it.

A couple of days later, staff from my department attended a colleague's leaving party. I didn't know the guy who was leaving very well. He worked up in the gate area. My colleagues knew him from when they worked in the gate area prior to joining the works department. I was invited to the party, but I decided against going. One, I didn't really know the guy, and two, the prospect of having a night out with Adam and Eve present just didn't do anything for me. Kieran from my department attended the party. Throughout the night, he texted me, informing me that Eve was slagging off Mitch and me a lot. She was calling me things from a pig to a dog; calling Mitch pretty much the same; and telling everyone how difficult she was going to make things at work for both me and Mitch. I still have all those text messages from Kieran. I had to have them printed out and sent to my legal team at a later date in case they were ever required for evidence.

Around ten days later, after Eve had upset things even more at work, Dick called her to his office and informed her that she was moving that day from the works department. She was to work as an escort outside of our department, this meaning that she would escort individual contractors who entered the prison and not the contractors in our department. Dick also informed Eve that she was not allowed in our department and was prohibited from having any contact with me and Mitch. This went down like a lead balloon. But now, both Adam and Eve were out of our department. There wasn't a lot either of them could do.

Funnily, over the next day or two, the rest of the team began to speak to Mitch and me. Within a few more days, they were all saying how much better it was with Adam and Eve gone. They began to admit that Adam and Eve were the trouble in the camp. They said that most of them had felt pressured and bullied by the both of them. After Adam and Eve were gone, the department became a much happier place and the job was getting done to the standard at which it should have been done. Even the contractors were happier.

Within only a day or two, the governor of the works department, Mr P, approached me as I was on my way into the prison and informed me that Adam and Eve would be returning to our department as soon as possible, as we were short-staffed. I argued the fact that they had only been out for a few days and that Dick had submitted the complaint against them and was looking into it, but this made no difference to

Mr P. He basically said that Adam and Eve were returning and that was that. When I caught up with Mitch that morning, I told him what Mr P had said to me. He was dumbstruck. I told Mitch that I had already encountered bullying in reception and that I wasn't prepared to encounter it again. We decided to go see Dick. As he was our manager and was already dealing with a complaint against both Adam and Eve, we would see what he could do. So we both went to pay Dick a visit. We expressed our concerns regarding Adam and Eve's return to our department, and then we asked him how the complaint was going. Dick informed us that nothing else would be done in regard to the complaint and that Mr P's decision to have Adam and Eve return to the works department would be the final decision.

I could not work under those circumstances, what with the continuous bullying from colleagues, and with management once again doing nothing about it. I had found myself back in the spot where I had been nearly two years prior. I did not go into work on the following day. At this stage, I was seriously thinking about whether I could continue to work alongside people who were a law unto their own and with managers who often swept important matters beneath the carpet.

Victimisation

Not very long before the incident with Adam and Eve, something else occurred in the works department. To this very day, I cannot get my head round it. Keith, the one I mentioned earlier who had worked in the prison's control room for many years, had joined us in the works department. He was one of the nicest fellas you could ever wish to meet. I believe he had about six years of employment left before he retired. He was looking forward to his retirement and to spending time with his wife and family. He had a wicked sense of humour. Almost every day, he would have us all in hysterics. The thing he did that made me laugh more than anything was when he would wear his peaked prison hat back to front and start rapping and dancing around the office. He would join us on nights out and for parties that we had. He and his wife had joined us on the weekend away we had in Sunderland. Keith was great fun, very down to earth and honest – just a truly lovely man. He also didn't take any crap off anyone. To Keith, a spade was a spade. He always spoke his mind and wouldn't let anyone intimidate or take the mickey out of him.

Tamwar and Keith always got on with each other. They would be partnered up quite often. In fact, at one time we in the works department named them "the Siamese twins", as they were assigned to a specific job within the prison and were on it together for months. They would leave the compound together each morning. They would lunch together, and they would return at the end of the day together. Then, all of a sudden, things changed slightly between them. The job they had been on together had finished, so they were both back in the compound escorting the usual contractors we had. I believe that Keith was beginning to see the relationship that Tamwar had with the managers. For instance, Tamwar's wife would make some delicious

Asian food. When Tamwar sometimes brought the food into the prison, he would hand it out to us in the works department. It was absolutely beautiful. The desserts his wife made were unbelievable. I loved it when he brought in food that his wife had made.

At one point, Tamwar began to bring in home-cooked Asian food for Dick, our manager, and for Chris, the manager who caused Mitch and me to be bullied. Tamwar, in all fairness, had a very close relationship with Dick and Chris. It worked for Tamwar, as a lot of the time he would get the cushy jobs. We his co-workers did believe that this was because of the relationship he had with management. Keith saw this as being unfair, as did most of my colleagues. I always liked Tamwar. I still do. I have contact with him now. I never saw his relationship with the managers as a major problem; however, I did believe that it was unfair to some of the others. I was in charge of the compound with Mitch, so he and I never went out to escort any contractors. I.e. the preferential treatment Tamwar received didn't affect us as such. Still, I could see how it could annoy other staff when Tamwar was given the inside jobs in the winter when the others would be standing outside for hours in the snow and the sleet. And, on occasions, Tamwar would leave the prison at lunchtime and not return for two hours or so. So Keith would pass comment. Like I said, a spade was a spade for Keith; he always spoke his mind. The comments I heard from Keith were things such as, "Tamwar gets what he wants cos he brings food in for management." Keith often brought up the fact that after we went to Sunderland, we had to prove that the contractors hadn't paid for us, as it would have been a conflict of interest and we would have been seen as having taken bribes if they had, yet Tamwar brought food in for management and that was fine.

Tamwar also had a wicked sense of humour, but in a different way from Keith. As the saying goes, if you see a lemon, squeeze it. Well, that was Tamwar's theory. So when Tamwar clicked onto the fact that his antics were annoying Keith, he played on it. He purposely said untrue things in front of Keith in the hope that Keith would believe them, which Keith did. For instance, when it was Christmastime, we staff each received a tin of chocolates from Governor Number One. Tamwar said that he had received two tins of chocolates for all of his good work and his consistency with timekeeping. This wound Keith up very much. Some of us told him not to take it all in, but Keith was having none of that. Then there was the time when Tamwar was going on holiday to Pakistan to visit his family but had no leave left. He had to apply for special leave or leave without pay or something, I can't quite remember. But he told Keith that the governor had granted him leave on full pay even though he had used all his annual leave. This was untrue, but Keith did believe Tamwar, as the latter was very convincing. Keith was getting more and more annoyed by the day. Then Tamwar really started to take the mickey. He decided to tell Keith that he was receiving special treatment because of his colour, something like reverse racism. This really got to Keith. It was sad, really, because Keith was the only one whom Tamwar targeted. The rest of us were all aware that Tamwar was on the wind-up, but Keith truly believed everything he said.

I never heard Keith say anything racist towards Tamwar. I must be honest and say that one particular morning when Keith was on milk duty, he had not brought in the milk. He turned to us all and said, "I was running late this morning and the Paki shop was shut." Keith was not directing that at Tamwar; he just said it in general to all of us. Declan had said this before in front of Tamwar and Tamwar had laughed at it.

Then things began to get worse. Tamwar was passing comments about how he got away with stuff because of his colour. This wound up Keith more and more. Then it was awkward when the two were partnered up again. A bad atmosphere developed between them. I believe things reached the stage where Keith would simply not speak to Tamwar.

One Monday morning after arriving at work, Tamwar looked at the rota and saw that he had been partnered with Keith. He decided to go see our manager, Dick, and ask if he could be partnered with someone else. Dick asked the reason for this. Tamwar said that he and Keith simply didn't get on anymore. Tamwar said that he would prefer to work alongside someone else. Dick asked if Keith had been racist towards him, and Tamwar clearly stated several times that Keith had not been racist towards him. He kept repeating that he just didn't get on with Keith. Dick had explained to Tamwar that if it was a case of racism, he would deal with it immediately, but Tamwar said that it was nothing like that and that he didn't want any kind of complaint to be made regarding racism. He didn't want an issue made of his request; he just wanted to swap partners. Dick asked if Keith had ever passed any racist comments. Tamwar told him what Keith had said that morning regarding the milk, but he admitted that it didn't bother him. He said that others had sometimes said things like that, but not intentionally. Dick told Tamwar to leave the matter with him.

Within one hour of Tamwar's going to see Dick, Keith had been asked to empty his locker and to hand in his radio, keys, and key chain. He was then escorted out of the prison. He had been suspended until further notice. Investigations began, with Dick and the other managers heading them up. Colleagues were interviewed under caution. The interviews were all recorded. Within a few weeks, Keith had his employment terminated. He would not return to the Prison Service. He lost his pension and his chance to serve the remaining few years before he retired. We in the works department were absolutely gutted over this. I believe that Tamwar was also saddened by the news.

There are two major points here that I am trying to raise. Firstly, I do believe that the matter between Keith and Tamwar was blown out of proportion and that the problem could have been quite easily solved without raising the issue of racism. My belief is that because of the relationship Dick had with Tamwar and because Dick didn't like Keith very much (or so I surmised; I have no idea why the former disliked the latter), Tamwar's request presented itself to Dick as an opportunity to get Keith out of the Prison Service. Secondly, there had been many prior complaints regarding Adam's bullying behaviour, but nothing was done about it. Mitch had gone to make a complaint against Adam. I was dragged into it thanks to the incompetence of Chris, which then led to bullying from Eve. I made a complaint against Eve, and Mitch had made a complaint against Adam, so those two were moved out of our department for a few days before we were told that they would be returning because the department was short-staffed. We were then told that nothing would be done regarding the complaint. Yet Tamwar visited Dick not even to make a complaint, but just to ask if he could swap partners, and within an hour Keith was suspended. Within a few weeks, Keith was sacked. Where is the fairness there? I believe this to be a case of victimisation.

I have not heard from Keith in quite a while now. However, not long after he had gotten the sack, he spoke with me. He couldn't stress enough to me that if management had it in for you, then you had no chance. He told me to be aware of how I was treated in light of what was going on with my brothers. He said that he had worked a lot of years in that prison and had seen many things. He said he had heard that management had it in for me because my brothers were arrested. I asked Keith why the managers would possibly have it in for me, as I had not done anything wrong and as my brothers had been on remand. Thereafter, one of my brothers had been found not guilty and the other was still awaiting trial. Keith said the managers were aware of my brother Willie and who he was. Apparently they didn't like him. Also, one or two of the older staff had come across Willie in their earlier employment within the Prison Service. Keith told me to always be aware, because they would try their best at any opportunity to get me out. I presumed that at this time Keith bore a huge grudge and was still hurting deeply because of how he had been treated by management and the Prison Service. Little did I know that everything he foretold was about to become reality.

Willie's Trial

While I was taking time off from work after I heard that Adam and Eve had been told that they would return to the works department, I went to seek advice from my solicitor. I was not in the union at work and clearly did not have a clue where I stood. I told my solicitor about what had occurred in the reception even though that had been dealt with. I also told him about the hassle I had endured regarding my brothers. He believed that the latter matter had been dealt with incorrectly. I told him about the incident with Adam and Eve, which he believed should have been investigated. He drafted me a letter to send in to my manager, Dick. The letter was sent from me, but it was my solicitor who had drafted it up. In the letter, we asked what Dick's intentions were regarding the incident with Adam and Eve. We also asked to be told the policies and procedures for a prison worker whose siblings were incarcerated. This letter was sent in the first week of January 2011. It is now April 2015, and I still haven't received the policies and procedures regarding a prison worker's incarcerated siblings. The appointment with the solicitor, the advice he gave, and the letter he drafted cost me and my husband £1,200.

After Dick received my letter, he contacted me at home and asked if he could come to see me at my home. I agreed to this in the hope that something would be done regarding Adam and Eve. I hoped that my and Mitch's complaint would be dealt with immediately, the same as Tamwar's had been dealt with, even though Tamwar's was not an official complaint. So the following morning, Dick attended my home. He was accompanied by Mr Bill. Mr Bill, the head of human resources, was known around the prison to be one of the worst members of staff. He was known as rude, ignorant, impolite, and arrogant. I never found this to be the case. Whenever I had seen him in and around the prison, he acknowledged me if I spoke to him or smiled at him. He didn't do this happily, but he would either say "good morning" or nod his head in acknowledgement. My husband was home on the day when Dick and Mr Bill attended. Mr Bill started the conversation by asking when I would be returning to work and if I was having any kind of problems within the workplace. It was apparent that Mr Bill was unaware of any issue regarding Adam and Eve. Dick had obviously not briefed Mr Bill about anything. After I explained to Mr Bill what had been occurring and, most of all, how things had come to reach this point because Chris omitted me and Mitch from the initial staff meeting, he was astounded. Dick was glaring at me when I was explaining to Mr Bill what had happened, giving me the "shut the hell up" look. Mr Bill asked Dick why he had not been made aware of this. Dick replied that it was all being dealt with. Dick looked very uncomfortable after he saw Mr Bill's reaction.

During this meeting, my husband brought up a few things with Dick and Mr Bill. One of the things was the time when Lester had tried knocking me over with the Category A wagon. Bruce said that the incident should have been captured on the prison camera. Dick looked at my husband and asked, "How do you know where my cameras are placed in the prison?"

My husband replied, "It is a top-security prison, I presume there are cameras all over."

Mr Bill smirked at Dick as if to say, "Ask a silly question ..."

Dick assured me that he would start to put things in place back at the prison in regard to Adam and Eve. He then said that he would be in touch with me as soon as possible. What he meant by "putting things into place", I didn't really know. Within a day or two, I was back in the prison and in Dick's office. Dick explained that Mitch and I would have no contact with Adam and Eve and that they would not return to the compound. He said that they would be used as contractor escorts outside the compound. Nothing else in regard to the complaint would be done, Dick said; he felt that was enough. He then informed me that I had a new manager. I wondered what he was on about, so I asked why there would be a new manager. He explained that our works governor, Mr P, was retiring in the next day or two and there was to be a change around. I asked who was going to be our new governor. He leant over his desk, looked at me real close in the face, and said, "Me." I smiled at him and asked how all this had come about. He said, "Well, Mr P is retiring, so I have taken promotion. I will now be works governor, which means we needed a replacement manager for me. I will call for him to come up to my office. I can introduce him to you." This he did. Within ten minutes or so, in came my new manager. I had not seen him before. This surprised me because Dick had told me that my new manager had worked in the prison for a number of years. I stood up, shook the man's hand, and introduced myself. He introduced himself as Darren. He told me that he had come from the prison kitchen and that it was all new to him becoming a works manager when he had been the principal officer in the kitchen for so long.

It then clicked to me who he was. I said, "Oh, you are the one that was leaving notes in the kitchen for me and my contractors asking us not to eat your bacon or you would have to kill us."

He laughed and said, "Oh yes. And you are the one that let your contractor eat Laurel's pack-up for court, aren't you?" Ha. We both laughed.

I don't think Dick liked the fact that we both laughing. He interrupted and said, "By the way, Darren, Liz's brother is on trial soon for importing Class A drugs into the country, so watch her." I looked at Dick in disgust.

Darren turned to Dick and said, "Well, I will support Liz in any way she needs." I liked him.

So, yes, Dick was correct, Willie's trial was fast approaching. Once again, it became the topic of discussion inside the prison. Officers would pass me by and say, "Not long now before he is going down for a lot of years" and "Have you bought your paper in bulk for all the letter writing you will be doing when he's gone down?" I heard comment after comment. I shrugged them all off, but they saddened me deeply.

March 2011 came around. The trial was looming. Willie wanted me to go to the trial, and I wanted to go myself. I knew after being turned down by security to attend Colin's trial that I had no chance, but I thought there was no harm in asking. I went to see Dick, who was my governor now. I would have asked my manager, Darren, but he probably would have told me to go without getting permission. I asked Dick if I could have permission to attend Willie's trial. He said to me, "I wouldn't have thought so, but I will contact security and ask them for you." It was a Mr Angler in security who dealt with these kind of issues now. The principal officer and the governor of security who had dealt with my visits had taken early retirement at this point. This was after many staff had snuck mobile phones had into the prison and given them to inmates; many SIM cards and phone chargers were found hidden in cells and in walls; and many female members of staff had had sex with inmates. So the two who had been in charge of security while those things were going on had now gone. Dick called me up to his office and claimed that he had spoken with Mr Angler. He said that, no, I could not attend the trial. Security would have a prison official in attendance at Willie's trial in case I did turn up. I thought that a little extreme, having a prison official in attendance. Plus, the trial wasn't local; it was in Middlesbrough. But I was told I could not attend. There was nothing I could do about it.

So the trial began. It was booked in for two weeks. On one of the mornings when I had gone through search and was putting my boots and other gear back on, an officer called my name. I turned round and saw about six or seven officers all looking into a little notebook type of thing. They said they were taking bets on Willie's verdict, guilty or not guilty. And because it the odds favoured a guilty verdict, they were taking bets on what sentence he would get. They said that twelve to fifteen years was coming in at 2 to 1. They asked me if I wanted to place a bet. I just walked away. I mentioned this incident to my colleagues. They told me to go see Dick, but what was the point? I thought I would just try to get the next two weeks out of the way. No matter what happened, the jibes, taunts, and insults would eventually die down. For the remainder of that week, it was pretty much the same. Officers carried on in the same manner, some of them asking me how the trial was going. I said nothing. Then one of my colleagues told me that he had been in a conversation that morning with Adam and Eve, who must have been asking my colleague if my brother was on trial that week. My colleague told them that he believed so. Eve turned round and said, "I really hope her brother gets found guilty and goes away for fifteen years."

My colleague said, "That's not very nice, Eve."

Eve replied, "Oh, it's not so Willie suffers. It's so Liz suffers. She loves her brother. If he is taken away from her, then she will suffer, so I can only hope he gets the maximum." Pure evil.

With only a day or two left of the trial, I received a phone call from Willie's barrister. He needed me to give some evidence regarding a phone call that Willie had made to me while he was on remand. It was quite imperative that I gave this evidence. Willie had already told his barrister that I was unable to attend the trial because the security department at my work had forbade me. When Willie's barrister spoke with me, he said it was absurd that I was not allowed to attend the trial. Even more absurd, he thought, was that I could not visit Willie in prison. The barrister said there was no law against this. He advised me to contact security again and to quote exactly what he had said. So I did this immediately. Mr Angler was not available, so I asked if a message could be passed to him. I quoted exactly what the barrister had said and then asked if Mr Angler could get back to me as soon as possible. Lo and behold, within the hour security came back to me and informed me that I could attend the remainder of Willie's trial, as long as I didn't stand up and give evidence. My evidence would have to be read out by Willie's barrister. I was also told to inform the prison immediately of the verdict.

I drove up to Middlesbrough the following day with my mum and my daughter, but I was too late to submit my evidence to the barrister, as the judge was summing up. He was summing up almost everything that happened that morning, definitely swaying towards the prosecution. In fact, when the jury went out, Willie's barrister said that if they came back with a guilty verdict, then Willie would have grounds for appeal because of how the judge had summed up. The barrister also said that if the jury came back with a guilty verdict, then the judge would pass sentence the following day and the sentence would be between twelve and fifteen years.

My mum, my daughter, and I went for lunch, but none of us really wanted to eat. We returned to the court at 2 p.m. The jury were still out. Willie's barrister came to see us and said that if the jury were much longer, then the trial would go on until the following day. We three were sitting and just waiting and waiting. Then the barrister came out and said the jury were coming back in. Willie gave us all a hug before he went in. He was fearing the worst at that point, as were we all. The arresting officers were all present in court. There were some unfamiliar faces too. Court had resumed. The spokesperson for the jury stood up and was asked, "Have you reached a verdict?"

She replied, "Yes." At this point, I was shaking from head to toe. Goodness knows how Willie felt. I put my head in my hands and waited.

She was then asked, "Do you find the defendant guilty or not guilty?"

She replied, "Not guilty."

I sat and sobbed. Then I stood and walked towards Willie, who was heading towards me. We put our arms around each other. He sobbed too. He said to me, "It's all over, love." Willie went straight over to the arresting officers, who were obviously gutted but who had to remain professional, and he shook their hands. He said to them, "I know you wanted the other verdict, and I know you have worked hard on this case."

One of the officers shook his hand and said, "Well done, Willie." The other officer stormed out of court. I, my mum, my daughter, and Willie were elated, overwhelmed, and full of emotion. I was relieved for Willie that the trial was over. I was also relieved that we were getting him back. And I had so much relief regarding the prison. My co-workers couldn't get at me anymore. They couldn't torment me by telling me how long Willie was going away for. I would no longer have to report to security about my movements. It was such a relief. I got on my phone and let the rest of my family know the outcome. It was too late to phone the prison, as my shift would have finished and most of the security staff would have left for the day. However, I did tell them that I would let them know immediately what the verdict was, so I phoned and left Dick a message. I then left security a message.

My family members were all standing outside the court, making phone calls, and just taking everything in. A couple of the jury members approached Willie and congratulated him. At this stage, I remembered that when the not guilty verdict was read, a jury member punched the air and shouted, "Get in." That was quite bizarre, really, as he would have been fully aware of the verdict. Ha.

My family then headed home. I dropped off my mum, and then the rest of us went to the pub and met up with other family members and friends.

When I returned to the prison, I was like a dog with two tails. I went straight to Dick's office and asked if he had received the message I had left, to which he replied, "Yes." He said nothing else, just "yes". I went to security and saw Mr Angler. I asked if he had received the message I had left. He replied, "Yes" – nothing else. My colleagues were pleased for me, especially Mitch, as he had seen how much my brother's predicament had affected me. I saw one or two of the officers who had taken bets on Willie's verdict and sentence. They completely blanked me. I asked one of them on approach if they had been taking bets on a not-guilty verdict, but he just glared at me. Word soon got around the prison. To be honest, I was just glad it was all over.

A day or two after I saw Eve in the prison grounds, we walked straight past each other in fact. She looked at me like I was a pile of turds she had just stood in. I thought about what she had said previous to my colleague about wanting Willie to be found guilty and receive the maximum sentence just so that it hurt me. I still couldn't believe that she wished that upon me. I know we had fallen out and would probably never speak again, but for her to have evil thoughts like that and to actually express them to other people was something that I found to be heartless, unkind, and pretty evil. A day or two later, I heard over the radio a call for Eve. She was asked to go straight to Dick's office. Her brother, who was an alcoholic, had died.

Good Cop, Bad Cop

After Willie's trial, I felt that things would be much better at the prison. Plus, I knew that Adam and Eve wouldn't be working in the compound, so that was a good thing. I had a new manager, Darren, and things were looking up. When I had first met Darren in Dick's office, I knew immediately that he and I would get on. I don't think many people liked Darren. Well, maybe it wasn't that they disliked him, but they found him to be a little annoying. He was very loud and used to come out with some absolutely classic statements. I believe that his character was one that just wound people up. I don't think he purposely would people up. It was just something about the way he was. I did hear rumours around the prison that the reason he had moved from his former prison to our prison was because he had let the inmates at the former prison walk all over him. Apparently he was allowing the inmates to place their own orders for food deliveries. As a result, that prison's food bills went sky-high. The inmates were eating luxurious meals and filling up their cells with goodies. How much truth there was to these rumours were, I am unsure. But to me, Darren was a star. Some staff said he was a liability within the prison and that his thinking sometimes was bizarre. I built up a wonderful working relationship with him though. Because Darren was new to the works department and didn't know our procedures, Mitch and I helped him with things that he was unsure about. Dick, on the other hand, would put Darren down if the latter got something wrong or said something that didn't make sense.

Throughout the new build of the kitchen, there were meetings held every Thursday morning. In attendance at these meetings were the managers from the works department, the governor of the works department (which was now Dick), the contracts managers, and sometimes officials from the home office. In one particular meeting where home office officials were present, the group were trying to establish how they could get a vast amount of concrete into the prison in just a short time. They were coming up with different ideas, like bringing in many wagons at the same time or somehow trying to get a special chute that could reach over the prison wall. All these ideas were useless, however, as security measures overruled. So Darren piped up and said, "Why don't we just knock a massive hole in the wall at the side of the football pitch?"

Apparently, the home office officials looked at Darren as if he had gone out of his mind. One of them said, "I don't think that is a very good idea, do you, knocking a hole in the wall right alongside where the inmates play football?"

"Well, it was just a thought," Darren said. "I am used to knocking a mean lasagne up, not working out how to get concrete into the nick." According to one of the contracts managers, when the home office officials had left, Dick gave Darren a right stripping down. But like Darren had said, he was used to cooking, not building, and it was all new to him.

Another time, a wagon had been brought into the prison. It was too high to get through the internal gates. The front end had gotten through, but because of the unevenness of the ground, the wagon had gotten stuck and couldn't move either forward or backward. The escorts had radioed me and asked me what they should do. I tried contacting Darren, but he wasn't responding to his radio or picking up the phone in his office. Neither was Dick. I presumed that the two were in a meeting, so I decided to go up to the works department. I would just have to enter the meeting. We couldn't leave the wagon like that; it needed sorting. When I arrived in the works department, I discovered that the meeting had just finished. Both Darren and Dick were standing behind the main desk. I looked at Darren and said, "Darren, we have a slight problem."

I began to explain about the wagon when Dick interrupted me, asking, "So why are you telling him?"

"Because he is my manager," I replied.

Dick looked at Darren and said sarcastically, "Go on then, Darren. I can't wait for this one."

Darren thought for a minute and said, "Well, from what Liz has said, I believe our only option is to let the tyres down on the wagon."

Dick looked at me and said, "See what I fucking mean? It's like asking a fucking brick."

"I will leave it with you then, Dick," I said. I headed back to the compound and was thinking that Dick had humiliated Darren.

An hour or so later, Darren came down to the compound. Before I had even unlocked the gate, I heard him shouting, "Guess what they have done? Let the fucking tyres down." He had a great big beam on his face. I felt sorry for Darren because he wasn't getting any help or guidance from any of the other managers or from Dick. All they did was take the mickey out of him and slag him off behind his back.

So Dick was now our governor. Within a few weeks, he had changed a lot of things. I think it had gone to his head very quickly that he had gotten the promotion and was now governor grade. He was a bit of an arse when he was a manager, but now he had become a lot of an arse. I don't think he liked the relationship I had with Darren. Whenever Dick slagged Darren off in front of me, I would stick up for Darren and would disagree with Dick. I also think that Dick hadn't liked it when he visited me at home and I had informed Mr Bill what had been going on at work. I also believe that Dick was one of those people who wished that my brother had been found guilty. Dick never, ever mentioned Willie's trial after I asked him if he had received my message regarding the verdict. Many people at work seemed to have plenty to say prior to the trial, but they said nothing about it afterwards. I thought maybe it was just me who thought that Dick had changed, but most of my colleagues said exactly the same thing about him: his promotion had gone to his head and he now thought he was God.

I began to notice that Dick rarely spoke to me or acknowledged me. On mornings when my colleagues and I were collecting keys and radios from the works department, more often than not we would all be there at the same time. Some mornings, Dick would be there helping to hand out the keys and radios. On many occasions, he spoke to my colleagues and to Mitch, but he very rarely spoke to me. Then I began to notice that Dick contacted Mitch on his works radio and gave him a message to pass onto me. It would have been much simpler and would have made more sense if Dick had contacted me on my radio instead of going through Mitch.

In October 2011, I had gotten a really bad cold that turned into the flu. I took two days' annual leave, as I did not want to go on sickness leave. Still not being very well, I went back into work. Around a week later, my condition was much worse. I had to attend my local A&E because I had severe chest pains. I stayed in hospital overnight and underwent tests and X-rays. I had dislodged my diaphragm because of the extent of my coughing. I was discharged from hospital the following day. Sent home with a course of antibiotics, I had been told to rest for the next few days. Before I was discharged, my husband contacted Darren to inform him of what was happening. Bruce told Darren that I wanted to use my own leave, as I had sufficient remaining. Darren told Bruce that that was fine. He sent his regards and best wishes to me. The following morning, Darren contacted me at home to ask how I was. He said that he had explained to Dick what had happened. Dick had told him that my absence had to go down as a sickness. I asked Darren why I couldn't use my own leave. He said that if it was up to him, he would allow it. He couldn't understand why Dick wouldn't allow it. So Darren told me that I had to self-certify for the next few days. I was well annoyed about this because I knew damn well that when Dick was our manager, he had allowed other staff to use their own leave when they weren't well.

Just prior to this incident, I had an appointment at the hospital to arrange for having surgery on my right eye. My right eye is artificial. The time had come for me to have surgery on my inner and outer lid. After I lived for many years without my right eye, the lid began to sag because it did not get the same amount of movement as the working eye did. The surgery is only minor, but it helps with the appearance and keeps the artificial eye more secure. My consultant told me that I would be waiting around six weeks for the surgery date, which gave me occasion to arrange time off from work. He told me that after my surgery I would need to be off work for approximately one week. This was purely because I would be unable to wear my artificial eye until the swelling went down and I had the stitches removed. I informed Darren after my consultation that I would require a week off work after the surgery. I asked him if I could use my annual leave. Darren told me that this was fine. In fact, I had built up toil (hours from working overtime). Seeing that I had built up quite a lot of toil, Darren said that I could use either those hours or my annual leave. A few days later, I was working late with some contractors who could only do the particular part of the job they were doing in the evening. It was just me, a dog handler, and

Darren who were working that evening. When we had finished, Darren pulled me to one side and asked me if I had upset Dick in any way. I told him, "Not that I know of," before I asked him why he asked.

Darren then told me that he had explained to Dick that I would be using either my toil or my annual leave when I went to have the surgery on my eye done. Dick had turned round to Darren and said, "Well, you can use your own discretion, Darren, and make her go on sickness leave. It is entirely up to you. But if I was you, I would make her go on sickness leave and not let her use her toil or annual leave."

Once again, I was well annoyed and asked Darren what he would decide by using his own discretion. He replied, "My discretion is to let you use your own leave, Liz. I wouldn't do that what Dick has said, and I can't understand why he has said that. That's why I ask you if you have upset him in any way, cos he seems to have it in for you." I spoke at length that night to Darren, telling him about the incident with Adam and Eve and telling him all about my brothers. I said that I felt that Dick had begun to treat me differently all of a sudden. Darren was very understanding and told me that I should not have been discredited for my brothers' imprisonment. He thought that this was even more the case when they were both found innocent. He also agreed that the incident with Adam and Eve should have been dealt with differently. He told me not to worry about Dick. I found that he had exactly the same theory as I did: if you go to work and do your job as it should be done, then you have nothing to worry about. I had always maintained that. There is nothing more simple than doing your job correctly and not doing anything underhanded.

Dick continued to be a little offhand with me, but as I had discussed with Darren, I just continued doing my job. Really, Dick's behaviour towards me went straight over my head.

One week, the works department was short-staffed. I think Darren had cocked up with the rota and with staff leave. I think he had allowed around five staff members off in the same week, when usually only two staff were allowed leave at one time. Because the department was short-staffed, some of the contractors said they would just work in the compound, either tidying up the tool sheds or asking the joiners to begin making particular things from the tool sheds. At this stage of the new build, I was running the compound myself. Mitch was running the actual compound where the new build was. In the compound where I was in charge, contractors normally needed an escort. We in the department never understood that rule, seeing as there was no way out for the contractor. I was the only keyholder of the compound. Plus, there were no inmates anywhere near or around the compound – and I was always there anyway.

So in the week when we were short-staffed and the contractors said they would work from the compound, I asked Darren if the contractors could work without an escort. I informed him that I would be present. Darren squared it with Dick first, and Dick said it was fine. Dick attended the compound a few times that week and saw clearly that a couple of contractors were working in and around the tool sheds. In fact, on one occasion, he talked for quite a while to the joiner, who was in and out of the tool shed and showing Dick different things. On the following day, it was only me and a joiner in the compound, as all of the contractors and escorts were out. The joiner was building something up just outside the tool shed, just as he had been doing the previous day when he was talking to Dick. I heard the compound gate rattling, so I went to unlock it. It was Dick and the new governor from the security department standing there. By all accords, the new governor was just doing random checks around the prison. I went into the office to book the both of them in. Within a second, Dick was calling my name, so I went out. Both he and the governor were standing by the tool shed where the joiner was working. The governor asked me why the tool shed was open and there was no escort with the joiner. I told him that I was the only member of staff in the compound and that I was looking after the joiner. He started shouting at me, saying, "You know there should be an escort with him. This is not on. Get the keys and lock this tool shed up immediately!"

I looked at Dick as if to say, "Come on, tell him the score."

Dick turned to me and said, "Governor is correct, Liz. You know the rules. Now go get the keys and lock the tool shed. And the joiner should have an escort with him. You know that."

The joiner was as fuming as I was. He said to the governor, "Hang on a minute. Why are you speaking to her like that? It's not her fault. She is only doing what she has been told to do." The governor and Dick weren't listening to him. I was dying to tell the governor that it was Dick who had sanctioned this set-up and that it was only the day previous when Dick had been standing in the very same place talking to the very same joiner with the very same tool shed unlocked. I decided against saying anything about it because I didn't want to drop Darren in it, seeing as we were short-staffed because of his error. So I kept my mouth shut. I went and got the keys and then locked up the tool shed. The governor checked everywhere else and said that all was OK. As the two men were leaving, Dick said to me, "May this be a lesson to you, Liz." The joiner was fuming and asked me why I hadn't said anything about the previous day. Once I explained to him that I hadn't wanted to drop Darren in it, he totally understood. Then, about an hour later, Darren came down to the compound and asked what had gone on. Both the joiner and I told Darren exactly what had happened. Darren was as bewildered as we were, but like Darren said, Dick would never admit to another governor that he had sanctioned this previously. He would sooner lay the blame on to me. Darren then told me that Dick had sent him down to the compound to give me a verbal warning.

I said, "You're having a laugh!"

He said, "No, I'm not, Liz. He told me to get straight down here and give you a verbal warning, but I am not going to. It is unfair when he was the one that sanctioned it and then humiliated you and made you take the blame, so he can shove his verbal warning up his fucking arse." Then Darren asked me why I hadn't said anything about Dick sanctioning the joiner's lack of an escort. I told him I didn't want to drop him in it since we were short-staffed. He smiled and gave me a wink. The incident had gotten the better of me though, so before I left the prison that night I called in to Dick's office and asked him why he said I had to have a verbal warning when it was he who had sanctioned the contractors working from the tool sheds.

He said, "I wasn't putting my hands up to that when I knew you would take the rap for Darren, your best buddy." I left his office and came to realise the fact that Dick definitely disliked the relationship I had with Darren. I believe that Dick wanted Darren to fail. However, while I and Mitch were there, that would not happen. We would not let that happen.

Leading up to Christmas 2011, there was not much getting done on the new build. This was simply because of the weather conditions. The temperatures were what determined whether the contractors would be in to work or not. If there weren't many contractors in, then the escorts would go elsewhere in the prison and Mitch and I would do full tool shed checks and do new inventories. On one particular day, it was pretty quiet, so Mitch and I said we would do some checks in the tool sheds. When contractors took their tools out in the morning, their escort would mark off the inventory the tools taken. At the end of the day, the contractors would return the tools to the sheds, at which time the escorts would add them back to the inventory. Mitch was going through the tools and I was counting them against what was marked on the inventory. Everything was tallying up until we got to the road pins. I had eight road pins on the list, but Mitch had counted only seven. There were no tools out that day, so we knew that it was not a case of the road pins having been taken out and an escort forgetting to remove them from the list. Mitch counted again and counted once again, but he still found only seven. So we turned that tool shed upside down looking for the eighth road pin, but to no avail. We looked through the other tool sheds to see if it had been put in there by mistake, but it hadn't. We knew this was a major security issue and knew it must be reported. But before making the report, we brought into the office the escorts and contractors who were working that day and told them the situation. We were trying to determine from the date the road pins had last been used and from the escort's signature where the road pins may have been used around the prison. The task was proving difficult. So Mitch and I decided to inform management first. Unfortunately, Darren was on leave that day, so we had to call for Dick to come down. When Dick came down, I took him to the tool shed. It was I, Drew, and Dick in the tool shed. I explained the situation. Dick looked on the inventory list to see who was the last escort to sign out the road pins. It was Tamwar. This did not prove that Tamwar had lost the road pin, but it didn't look good. I said to Dick, "What do we do now? We have searched everywhere and can't find it."

Dick got a tissue out of his pocket, wiped the number eight off the inventory, and wrote the number seven in its place. "Sorted," he said.

Mitch and I looked at each other in disbelief. I said, "You can't do that."

Dick said, "I can do what I want. I am a governor."

"Yes," I said, "but that missing road pin could be anywhere in the prison. If it gets into the hands of an inmate, not only are inmates in danger, but staff too." I was panicking. Mitch didn't say much. I think he was just gobsmacked.

"Like I said," Dick replied, "I can do what I want." He left the compound without saying another word. Mitch and I were left speechless.

Back in the office, I and my co-workers agreed that if we took the matter higher, then Dick would deny doing what he had done and would just say that nothing was missing, that the tools had added up with the inventory. The rest of the staff didn't want to get in trouble or have to be retrained. Tamwar definitely didn't want any repercussions. So they all agreed to keep quiet about the missing road pin. But I had a major problem. I could not have lived with myself if a member of staff or an inmate was attacked or, even worse, severely beaten with this road pin. This road pin was obviously floating around the prison somewhere. Yes, it could still be lying in the grounds somewhere, unseen and unfound, but it could also have been picked up by an inmate and hidden somewhere for when the time was right. I did not know the best approach to this situation. Dick already had it in for me. My colleagues didn't want me to come forward. I spoke with my Mitch and told him my feelings about the situation. He was in full agreement but was also unsure what we should do. Then I came up with a mega idea.

There is a system in the prison where you can make an anonymous report about a serious incident. To do this, one filled in a form and put the form inside a box. These boxes, for anyone to use, were dotted all around the prison. Staff, inmates, civvies, anyone, could put a serious-incident report in a box. At the end of each day, these boxes were emptied and all of the reports were taken up to security. The forms did ask for a signature, but I believe that the majority of these reports went in unsigned for reasons similar to mine.

Mitch and I filled in a form, writing that a road pin was missing from the works department. We didn't mention how we were aware of this. Neither did we write down that Dick had changed the number of road pins on the inventory. We just simply reported that a road pin was missing from the works department. We didn't sign the form; instead, we put it in as anonymous. We actually placed it in one of the boxes that was situated in the same building that housed the security department. This was one of the prison's main boxes. Both Mitch and I agreed that when security emptied the box, which would probably be that very night or, at the latest, the following morning, they would discern that the report form could have been placed there by any member of the works staff, as all of the staff in our team were fully aware of what had happened. So Mitch and I weren't too worried. My priority was making sure that the road pin was found before any damage was done to either staff or inmates.

The following morning when Mitch and I went to open the compound, we were half expecting the tool sheds to be turned upside down. We had even imagined that we wouldn't be permitted to enter that area on account of a missing tool in the prison. But everything was quiet and normal. Mitch commented that security could be arrive at any time, either that morning or later in the day. They never came. Neither did they come the following day or the following week. The road pin went missing in 2011. It is now 2015. I honestly believe that the road pin is still somewhere in that prison, in the wrong hands.

Prewarned

After Willie's trial, I presumed that all would be well at the prison. But it was around that time that Dick seemed to change towards me. I thought he had changed because he became a governor and the higher grade had gone to his head. A few of the staff had commented on his change of attitude. But I found out the real reason for his change once a friend of mine said to something about it to me on the quiet. Molly, a friend of mine who works in another local prison but not the same prison as I worked in, used to meet up with me from time to time. She knew my brothers Willie and Colin, as she had known my entire family for many years. In fact, when I was a young girl, Molly and her partner lived next door to us. We go back a long time. She is quite a close family friend. Molly's brother was a prison officer at the prison during the same time I worked there. I saw him in the prison now and then, and he would always acknowledge me. I didn't know him as well as I knew Molly, but he knew who I was and was always polite to me, unlike a lot of the officers there.

When my brothers were on remand, Molly often asked after them, asking about their progress and so on. But she kept emphasising to me that the staff at the prison were sure to have it in for me on account of my brothers' being on remand. She often told me to make sure I let the prison know when I was visiting my brothers and let them know about any updates regarding my brothers, such as any court dates they had. Telling me that anything the prison could pull me for, they would, she suggested that I not give them the chance. I did do everything by the book when Willie and Colin were remanded – and afterwards too – but I took the advice that Molly gave me. I double-checked everything. After both of my brothers had been on trial and had both received the verdict of not guilty, Molly was pleased with the news. Still, she told me to be on my guard at work (excuse the pun). During the time when Dick had become governor of the works department and Darren was my manager, I was out in my local pub and had met up with Molly for a drink and a catch-up. She said she had something to tell me, but she didn't want it going any farther, as she was fully aware of what the prison was like and didn't want any repercussions for herself or for her brother. It is purely academic now, as both Molly and her brother are now retired. That night, she told me that her brother, who worked in the same prison where I worked, had told her that the staff were trying to get me out of the Prison Service. They didn't like the fact that I had visited my brother Colin in prison or the fact that I had attended Willie's trial. They were even unhappier about the fact that both of my brothers had been found not guilty. I said to Molly that this was bizarre, given that my brothers were innocent. Even if they had been found guilty, I had never done anything wrong in my entire life. She told me that her brother had said that the staff were trying to set me up with something at work so that I would be sacked. I couldn't believe it. "Why? Why would they possibly want to do that?" I got really upset that night and kept asking Molly why the staff would possibly want to do that to me. Her brother had said that it wasn't directly me they didn't like; it was my brother Willie they had a problem with. But why take it out on me? I was furious. Then I began to think about things that had happened at work. For instance, the chub lock that Dick had in his drawer – was there a plan for that to come back on me? Missing keys that colleagues had misplaced – were they going to come back on me? Luckily, I was either off shift or on annual leave when those incidents occurred, so they could not have come back on me. The incident with the contractors working from the tool sheds and my getting a verbal warning – was that part of the plan? Then the worst thing, the road pin. Holy smoke. I began thinking that something was going to come back on me, that I would get the blame for some six-foot-six convicted murderer's getting hold of a road pin. Then I had to see sense and come to terms with the idea that I was being paranoid. I resolved that all I had to do was do my job correctly and I would be OK. But it is very difficult to believe this when managers and governors are doing wrong and covering up their wrongdoings. In such a situation, staff fear speaking up because they fear repercussions. Molly simply told me to be very careful at work, because the staff were out for me and would probably try anything to get rid of me. But she had the same theory as I did: if I did nothing wrong, then they couldn't get me.

I remember that the prison officers at the prison where my brothers had been held commented to my brothers that I was treated unfairly in regard to my visiting them and so forth. They had said that if I had worked at their prison, then I would have been treated differently from what I had been at the prison where I worked. They were even aware of how bad the staff were where I worked. They knew that a lot of the officers were prehistoric and behaved like dinosaurs. They passed the comment that my life would be made a misery. But what about Dick? His son was away for committing sex crimes. Why wasn't Dick treated the same as I was? Oh yes, he was a manager and then became a governor, so he was OK.

Now all I could focus on was going to work and doing my job correctly, the same as I had done for the whole time I had worked there. But I was more vigilant than ever before. I double-checked everything. I scrutinised identification tags when staff and contractors were entering the compound. Sometimes there would be covert operations, e.g. a dodgy ID would be put on a person. The ID might display the person's photo, but the name might have been changed to Donald Duck or something ridiculous like that, just to see if staff were doing our jobs correctly. I was in total agreement with this type of procedure, as one can't be letting any Donald Duck in or out of a prison. But I became extreme with the ID checks. Some of the contractors or staff would look at me as if I'd gone out of my mind because I took such a long time to scrutinise the IDs. But I thought that the smallest mistake could have been lethal for me. If any of my colleagues had let someone through with a false ID, then he or she would have to be retrained, but if I had let someone through with a false ID, then I probably would have faced disciplinary action.

During this time when I was extra vigilant, there was another incident in the works department – well, in the compound, actually – and this one was a massive security breach. All of my colleagues were out escorting, Mitch was over in the other compound where the new build was, and I was in the main compound. Not long into the morning, Tamwar returned to the compound and was in a right state. He had lost his radio! How this had happened was beyond me. The prison radio is like gold. As soon as you have signed for your radio in the morning or whenever you have gone on shift, the radio is attached to you and remains attached until it is signed out at the end of your shift. Losing or misplacing a radio is a massive security breach for obvious reasons. If a radio falls into the hands of an inmate, then the inmate can listen in to the goings-on around the prison or work out the codes used by staff, or even strip the radio and use the mechanisms for other devices the inmate may be trying to build.

I told Tamwar to calm down and to try to remember when he had last used his radio. He had been out with contractors around the prison and over at the new build and was coming back to the main compound just to change his boots. It was while he was heading back to the compound that he realised his radio wasn't in his possession. I told him to go retrace his tracks and to go everywhere he had been that morning. This he did, but to no avail. We had no option but to report the matter immediately. This wasn't an incident where we could waste any more time looking for the radio. It was a major incident that had to be dealt with straightaway. I contacted Darren and asked him to attend the compound immediately. Tamwar informed Darren of the missing radio as soon as the latter entered the compound. Darren turned to Tamwar and asked, "What the fuck have you done? Do you realise what this means, you thick bastard?"

I said, "That's it, Darren. Make him feel better than he already does." Tamwar was devastated. I think he had gone in to shock. He couldn't speak. He looked like he was in a daze.

Darren contacted Dick. Dick said, "Well done, Darren. Another cock-up," as if it were Darren who had lost the radio. Then the missing radio was reported immediately to security. Within minutes, all movement in and around our department had been ordered to stop. Contractors had to stop work and be escorted back to the compound. All escorts were called back to the compound. There was to be no more movement. The DST (dedicated search team) were down within minutes. They started a full search of the compound. Then they moved to the other compound and did a full search there. Then they escorted Tamwar through all his movements that morning, asking him where he had been, whom he had escorted, and when the last time that he had used his radio was. The prison was almost turned upside down, but it was all to no avail: no radio to be found. The only positive was that Tamwar had not been in the main jail and had not been on any of the wings or near the inmates' association area or exercise yards. But he had been around the inmates' football pitch. DST searched everywhere. The dogs were out searching. Everyone was searching, but still no radio. It was a complete mystery as to where it went, as it is very hard to lose or misplace a radio in a prison. A radio should be able to be detected wherever it may be in case of hostage situations and the like, but this one couldn't even be detected. It was like it never existed.

Work stopped all that day. The contractors were going mad since they were on a schedule, but nothing could be done. What had happened was a major incident. All of us in the works department had to write statements that day, stating our every movement from the time of our entering the prison up to the time of Tamwar's reporting the loss of his radio. This took up the rest of my day, as all of my colleagues except for Mitch and Drew asked me to write their reports for them (they would then sign them). They all liked my handwriting and said I could spell much better than they could. So one by one, they all gave me their statements in rough shorthand. I wrote them all out for them, after which time they read and signed them. On our way out of the prison, we were all subjected to an exit search. Tamwar was told to appear in the deputy governor's office on the following day. All of our team presumed that Tamwar would have to face disciplinary action, figuring that he might be retrained or be suspended. Even Tamwar was expecting the worst.

The following morning, Tamwar was up in the deputy governor's office. After he was given a verbal warning, the incident was over. When Tamwar returned to the compound, he told me that he wanted to speak to Darren but couldn't get hold of him. I tried contacting Darren by phone and by radio, but he did not respond. Tamwar went up to Darren's office, but Darren wasn't there. He was nowhere to be found. I saw one of the joiners walking by the compound, so I shouted to him and asked if he had seen Darren anywhere. He replied, "Oh, he has gone down to the segregation unit to ask if Bronson can be released on Christmas Day." Bizarre! I don't know if this was true. Knowing Darren, I figured that there could have been some truth in it.

Eventually, we were able to find Darren. Tamwar went to see him and told him that he thought he had been set-up. He knew that some staff and even some contractors disliked him after Keith got the sack after being accused of racism. Tamwar thought that someone was out to get him. He commented that he remembered a skip wagon being in the new build compound prior to his radio's going missing. He thought that someone had somehow gotten his radio and thrown it in the skip wagon just before the wagon left the prison. I am unsure if there could have been any truth in this claim, but it was very strange that the radio was not found in the prison even after the extensive searches were done. Tamwar was upset over the whole situation and was told to go home on full pay. He went on sickness leave (with stress) the following day and was told that because he thought he had been set up, he should have a good think over the next couple of weeks to determine whether or not he would like to be moved to a different department, one where he would feel more comfortable.

It was always at the back of my mind the warning that Molly had given to me and what she had said to me about getting set up. Part of me did think that Tamwar could have been set up, but then part of me told me that he wouldn't have been sent home on full pay or given the option to move departments if management were trying to set him up. It all seemed strange to me, but I decided, just like Molly had said, to do things correctly so that all would be well.

Speaking of Charlie Bronson and about Darren's visit to the segregation unit, I have many thoughts about Charlie. I had heard many stories about Charlie from staff at the prison. Most of these stories were overexaggerated and blown out of proportion. And of course the media have said many things about Charlie. Known to most people as one of Britain's most notorious criminals, Charlie Bronson spent many years incarcerated, most of those years in solitary confinement. Yes, Charlie has attacked prison staff and inmates and also destroyed prison property. However, it is my opinion that the reason for Charlie's behaviour is the fact that he endured years and years of solitude. First imprisoned in 1974 for an armed robbery (he stole less than thirty pounds and received a sentence of seven years), Charlie has, since that time, been held in many different prisons and served most of his time in solitary confinement. He never murdered, killed, or raped anyone, yet he spent many years behind bars.

I came close up to Charlie only once while I was at the prison. I had to take some contractors into the segregation unit. Once I entered the unit, the officers on shift told me that Charlie was out of his cell and was in a cage, exercising on an exercise machine. I asked if it was OK for me and the contractors to go to that area, as the contractors needed to take some measurements there for future works. The officers told me that I could, but they said that as I was wearing a high-visibility waistcoat, Charlie would snarl and try get to me, as he hated the colour yellow. I told the officers I would remove my waistcoat, but they said I couldn't go down to that area without it on. So off I went, down towards Charlie. He was out of his cell and was exercising. As I approached, he turned to look at me. I was afraid that he would kick off when he saw my high-visibility waistcoat, but his response was the total opposite. He gave me a big, lovely smile and said in his cockney accent, "All right, darling." I looked at Charlie, smiled, and said hello to him.

My thoughts were with Charlie every day at that prison and also when I was away from the prison. On some very early mornings at the prison, the binmen would purposely make as much racket as humanly possible near to Charlie's cell just to goad and annoy him. I would often hear Charlie shout to them to stop making all the racket. I could never understand where Charlie got his tolerance from, given all his years in prison, all the goading he endured, and all the time he spent in solitude.

On one occasion, there was an incident in the prison. We were told that Charlie had kicked off while exercising. The DST had been called to go sort him out. I believe that Charlie had been given some bad news regarding his parole and had kicked off. I don't know this for a fact, as one couldn't believe anything that anyone said in that place. I don't know how the incident ended. Upon leaving the jail that day, Mitch and I were walking behind the DST and heard them talking about the incident with Charlie. One of them said, "Yeah, he thinks he's fucking hard. But once I sprayed the pepper spray, he fell to the floor like a bag of fucking shit."

It really wound me up to hear how the DST were bragging about what had happened. I commented to Mitch quite loudly behind the DST, "Wonder how many of them would go in with Charlie alone without the pepper spray?"

Charlie has won awards for his writing and his artwork. He has done much work for charity, including setting up a children's charity. Many people do not see that side of Charlie. Instead, they listen to the horror stories told by officers who have probably bullied Charlie. Far worse and more-dangerous prisoners than Charlie have been released or have enjoyed better living conditions within the prison system. For example, some of them have been allowed to have televisions and PlayStations, have been allowed to associate with other prisoners and to play pool, and have benefited simply by not being alone.

It is my opinion that Charlie should be given the chance to prove that he is safe to be released. He should be given the opportunity to spend the remainder of his life with his wife-to-be, his family, his friends, and the people who love him and care for him.

The Key to Out

Christmas 2011 had come and gone. We were into another new year. Dick was still being an arse to me, but it was nothing to write home about, just his usual ignorance towards me. Everything was going OK at work, apart from a couple of happenings on the other side. When I say "the other side", I mean the spiritual side. Not everyone believes in the other side and a lot of people remain sceptical about it, but I am a big believer in it.

Every morning, religiously, Mitch and I would meet in the car park and enter the prison together. On one particular morning, Mitch was on annual leave, so I entered the prison on my own. I had gone through search and was collecting my keys. The senior officer who was on duty that morning, Alan, was some kind of clairvoyant/medium. In his spare time, he held psychic meetings and did some kind of clairvoyance sessions. I had just collected my keys when Alan said to me, "Good morning, Liz. I see he is with you again."

I thought Alan was being sarcastic regarding Mitch's not being at my side, so I said, "Oh, he is on annual leave today."

"No," he said. "I mean your dad. He is with you again this morning."

I went cold. My dad had been dead for twenty years at this point. "What do you mean?" I asked him.

He said, "Your dad comes in every morning with you. He stands at the back of you, and he leaves with you at the end of the day. He looks out for you and keeps you safe, but he has told me to tell you to watch your keys."

"Watch my keys?" I thought. I immediately looked down to my keys. They were safe and secure. What Alan had said made me shiver, but in the same sense it made me feel at ease.

A day or two after this, with the end of shift approaching, all of the contractors had left the compound, as had the escorts. Mitch was still on annual leave, so Bill had been in charge of the new build compound. It was getting dark. I was all ready to do the final locking up and the final checks. Bill was now in my compound and was helping me to lock up. Above my office was another office from where the contracts managers worked. Many a time when I was alone in the compound, I would hear footsteps walking across the office floor above me, even when there was no one up there. Mitch had encountered these happenings too, but neither Mitch or I was scared. It never bothered us. So Bill was locking up the offices and I was locking up the toilets and canteen. The toilet block was opposite the offices, about twenty yards away. I had checked the toilet block and was just locking it up when I heard Bill shouting, "Oh, are you locking up there, Liz?" Bill was standing outside my office and looking up towards the managers' office. Then he turned and saw me walking away from the toilet block. He went drip white and ran towards me while shouting, "What the fuck, what the fuck?!"

I asked, "What's wrong, Bill?"

Shaking like a leaf, he said, "I could hear you walking in the office above, and I heard you use your keys. That's why I shouted up to you, to ask if you were locking up. Then I turned round and saw you coming away from the toilet block. Who the fuck is up there? Is there someone still here?"

I said, "No, Bill, there is no one up there."

He began to get irate. "I am telling you, there is someone up there. I am not lying, Liz. I can hear them."

"I know," I said. "We have heard it before. But everyone has left, Bill. There is no one up there." Bill was convinced that there must have been a manager still up there – or a staff member or someone else. I said to him, "Well, we still have to lock up there, so we will go double-check now." I could see the fear in his face. He made me go up the steps first. I was dying to laugh. I would have thought that the man would have gone first.

As we approached the office door, Bill said, "Are you going in there unarmed? It could be an inmate hiding in the filing cabinet or something like that." I opened the door and went in. Bill followed. We had a look about. We found no one there, but I already knew that. I locked up the office. Just as we were approaching the outside steps, we both heard the footsteps in the office and the jingling of keys. There were eighteen steps to go down. I think that Bill took them in two strides, screaming, "Fuck me, fuck me, fuck me. Get me fucking out of here!" Bill vowed that he would never go up to that floor ever again and that he would never be alone in the compound ever again. The main compound and the one remaining building there used to be the prison morgue. There had been many hangings in the prison before hanging was abolished. Also, the prison graveyard was previously located at the side of the morgue, which was exactly the place where Bill and I had been located in the prison. I don't know if Bill was aware of this, but I made him none the wiser.

On 11 January 2012, Mitch and I had gone into work and done our usual routine. I never believed in a million years that this would be one of the last days I would work in the prison. Mitch and I had gone through search, collected our main prison radios and main prison keys, and arrived in the works department at around 7.25 a.m. This is where we would collect our internal radios and the keys required for use in the compound. These keys were for the contractors' vehicles, such as dumper trucks, forklifts, and cherry pickers, and also for tool sheds, toilets, the canteen, and so forth. Part of the routine, which had been the same routine for the ten months previous, was that the manager who was issuing the keys and radios for the day would remove the keys from the key safe and place them on the counter. Either Mitch or I would check that each key was present, usually key numbers 12 to 21, then either one of us would sign for the keys. The keys would then be put into a thick cloth prison bag. We would also sign for our internal radios.

On this particular morning, Chris was the manager issuing the keys and radios, the same Chris who had omitted Mitch and me from the staff meeting about Adam and Eve and who had caused us to endure bullying. The keys had already been put into the prison bag – for what reason I do not know. Chris had put the keys into the prison bag and said they were all present. While I was signing for my radio, I heard Mitch say, "I have checked the keys, Liz," so I did our usual routine and signed for the keys. Mitch then took the bag of keys from the counter and put them straight into his prison-issue bag. We left the works department and walked down to the compound. Mitch and I entered the office. Within a minute or so, our colleague Drew entered the office. I unlocked the key safe in the office and asked Mitch if he would pass me the bag of keys out of his bag. This he did. Drew was making a brew at the other end of the office. I emptied the bag of keys onto my desk and I knew straightaway that key number 19 wasn't there. I knew this because that particular key had a different tally colour from the rest of the keys, so it always stood out. I looked through all the keys and still found that key number 19 was not there.

I said to Mitch, "I thought you said you had checked the keys, Mitch. Number 19 is missing."

Mitch replied, "No. I thought you had checked the keys."

What had happened was this: when we were in the works department collecting the keys and radios, I had heard Mitch say, "I've checked the keys, Liz." He had actually said, "Have you checked the keys, Liz?" It had been a misunderstanding. Chris had said that the keys were all present and correct. The number 19 key was not in the bag, I found when I emptied the bag. Drew came straight over to my desk to see what was wrong. He also saw that the key was not there. Mitch went straight back up to the works department to see Chris. Chris said to Mitch that he had put all the keys into the bag. Mitch asked why he had put the keys in the bag. He told me later that Chris didn't answer him except for to smirk. Both Mitch and Chris had a look in the key safe in the works department where Chris would have taken the keys from. They also looked around the counter area, but to no avail. Chris told Mitch to go back to the compound and look again, but like Mitch said, it was pretty pointless because the key was not in the bag when it was emptied. When Mitch returned to the compound, I told him that we would have to report the missing key to our line manager, Darren. Mitch went to use the telephone in the upstairs office and phoned Darren to report what had happened.

Key number 19 was the key for the mini-dumper, so we knew that the next priority was to get the dumper out of the prison and, thereby, make the prison safe. By 9 a.m., the dumper had been taken out of the prison. While it was being escorted out of the prison, I was still looking around for the key, not that I was going to find it anywhere in the compound. But then I wondered how the dumper had been started up without the key. I asked the escort who had taken the contractor and the dumper out and how the dumper had been started. The escort informed me that the dumper had been started using another vehicle key that apparently fit the dumper's ignition. I was unaware of this. When I mentioned it to Darren, he said that he and Dick were fully aware that some vehicles could be started with other vehicle keys. Well,

I found this unbelievable. Why would we have keys that started up different vehicles? What, then, was the point of accounting for each key to each vehicle?

Later that morning, Darren came down to see me and told me that he had reported the incident to security. He said that security had informed him that because I was the one who signed for the keys, I would be responsible for the one that had gone missing. I explained to Darren that no way was that key in the bag and that Chris, for some reason, had already put the keys in the bag and then had told me and Mitch that they were all present and correct. Darren looked at me for ages and ages. I asked, "What?"

He said to me, "Someone may have it in for you, Liz." With the key incident happening so quickly, I had never stopped to think about much. But then it suddenly dawned on me: I had been set up! Darren sympathised with me and said he felt for me because of my work situation. He then asked me to write a statement to give to security. He said that Mitch would be required to do one too.

Once again, the job had been stopped. Everyone, including escorts and contractors, had been called back to the compound until DST had been through. I was explaining to the contractors what exactly had happened that morning and how the key was not in the bag once I emptied it. Every one of the contractors said the same – that I had been set up – as did the contracts managers and my colleagues.

Just after lunch, the DST arrived at the compound and asked Mitch and me to tell them exactly what had occurred that morning. Darren was also present with us. The DST did a thorough search of the compound and the office, then Mitch and I were subjected to a Grade A search. This was not just a routine pat-down search. It was the full search: belts off, jumpers off, boots and socks off, pockets emptied, etc. The DST then commented that it should be the works department they should be searching, as the team also thought that the key had not even entered the compound.

Darren asked if Mitch and I had finished our statements for security. We were only halfway through, so he waited for us to finish the statements. Once we completed them, he left along with the DST. All that afternoon, I was wondering what would happen next. My colleagues assured me that I would be OK and kept reminding me that both Declan and Bill had lost a key and they didn't even get a verbal warning. They recalled that Tamwar had gotten only a verbal warning after what he had lost. I knew that my colleagues were right, but I was very annoyed that the matter didn't entail merely a key that had been misplaced or accidentally dropped down a grate or something. I honestly believed I had been set up, and so did everyone else.

After the shift had finished, both Mitch and I were fully aware that we would have to have an exit search upon leaving the prison even though we had both had a body search earlier in the afternoon. And a search was never straightforward for me, anyway. If you walk through the portals and don't bleep, then you just go through, but I bleeped each time as I have a magnet stitched into my eye socket to aid the movement of my artificial eye. Every time I bleeped, I was subjected to a full rub-down. Mitch and I began our walk up to the search area. When we were about halfway up, we heard Darren shout at us, telling us to wait for him. On the way up to the gate area, Darren informed me that from 8 a.m. the following morning I had to report to the gate area for gate duties. He said that I could no longer work in the works department. I was suspended from the works department and was also under investigation. I went straight into a state of shock. I could not comprehend what he was saying. He kept repeating to me that it was not his decision, that it had come from security, that it was Mr Angler who had made the decision. I could hear Mitch saying that they couldn't do that to me, and I could just hear Darren saying that it was nothing to do with him, that it had come from security. By this time, Mitch and I had reached the key chute area. Lo and behold, I was asked to ready myself for an exit search. Just me, not Mitch. So I had to go the opposite way from Darren. I didn't get the chance to speak any more with him, not that I could speak, really. I was in shock. As I was placing my belongings into the search tray, I looked around and saw that Chris was just about to walk past me. He looked straight into my eyes and laughed in my face. When I was going through the exit search, two members of staff commented to me that I was on their detail for the next day. They asked me what I had done wrong to be suspended from the works department. I couldn't even speak to them; no words would come out of my mouth. Apparently, my name had been on their detail since 1 p.m., yet my manager had only just informed me at around 3.40 p.m. on my way out of the prison. I managed to look on the detail, and, yes, my name was there. I was down for gate search in the morning.

The worst insult was that I was down for secure waste in the afternoon. That was basically collecting used adult nappies from the healthcare department, and used syringes and used condoms from the wings. It was the worst job in the prison.

When I got through the exit search and was outside the prison, Mitch was waiting for me. We walked to the car park. I remember sitting in Mitch's car for a while with him until I had gotten my bearings back. We were both gobsmacked. Mitch said to me, "Liz, they can't put you in the gate area. It is a hostile area for you to work after the reception bullying. And can you imagine having to search Adam and Eve when they come through?"

I looked at Mitch and said, "I can't take this anymore. They have wanted me out for ages. I should have known something like this would happen. How can they do this to me when all I have ever done is my job right, yet others get away with blatant incompetence?" We sat there for quite a while before I said to Mitch, "You know I am never going back in that prison again, don't you?" He nodded his head and said nothing. I said goodbye to Mitch, got in my car, and drove home. I don't even remember driving home that night. It was all oblivion.

When I arrived home, Bruce was still at work, so I sent him a text message. I couldn't speak on the phone. I asked him to come home as soon as he could. He told me afterwards that he knew straightaway that something bad had happened at the prison. When he came in the house, I just sat and cried. I couldn't tell him for ages what was wrong. Eventually, I calmed down and told him everything that had happened that day. He was furious. I told him that I had had enough and that I could not continue being treated in that way – from reception to my brothers to Adam and Eve, and now this. It was as if I was doomed. Bruce told me to quit my job. He said it wasn't worth the grief, the heartache, the hair loss, the stress. Bruce commented that I hadn't mentioned Dick's name. This was because Dick hadn't been at work that day. Then we both clicked on at the same time: it was most probable that Dick had set me up along with Chris. Dick took the day off and got Chris to remove a key, knowing that I would be held liable for it. Dick was out of the picture in case anything went wrong. That was my and Bruce's belief, and it remains our belief. My suspicion was supported by the way that Chris laughed in my face on my way out of the prison and by the fact that Chris omitted Mitch and me from the staff meeting about Adam and Eve – and that Dick did nothing about it. It was all fitting together, including Molly's telling me that the staff at work were trying to set me up in order to get me out. I was absolutely gutted about the whole situation.

The following morning after a sleepless night, I phoned Darren and left him a message, as he mustn't have been in his office. I told him that I would not be in work that day and that I was contacting the Prison Officers' Association (POA) to see where I stood after what happened the day before. I had joined the POA after the incident with Adam and Eve in case anything else occurred. I tried contacting the POA, but I couldn't get hold of them. I tried and tried again, but still to no avail. Then Darren phoned me and said that I shouldn't have contacted him, as he was no longer my manager. He said that I should have contacted the senior officer in the gate area. I told Darren that I thought it was very unprofessional of him to tell me on our way out of the prison that I was under investigation and was suspended from my job. I also told him that the gate area was a hostile area for me to work in. He said that he hadn't realised this. I ended up arguing with Darren that morning on the phone. I had never argued with anyone at work. My colleagues told me that I was the most placid person they had ever met. But on this particular morning, tensions were running high and Darren was really annoying me. I said to him, "Darren, it doesn't really matter to me right now whether you are my manager or whether the senior officer from the gate is my manager. I am not coming back into that prison until I have spoken with the POA." We left it at that. He said he would get back to me.

I continued with trying to get hold of the POA, but still no joy. Why pay subs to the POA only to find that when you need them, you can't find them? Darren phoned me back and said that because I had not phoned in sick and had not been granted annual leave, he was putting me down as AWOL. He said that the senior officer from the control room had contacted Darren and asked where I was, as all the staff were accounted for except for me. Darren had explained that I had phoned in and was awaiting to speak with the POA. This wasn't good enough. I either had to be on annual leave or sickness leave; otherwise, I would be classed as AWOL. Darren explained that if I went down as AWOL, then they could send a prison official out with a police officer to arrest me. He said I had until midday to get back to him. This was going from bad to worse. I had visions of myself sitting handcuffed in a police cell. I couldn't get through to the POA, so I phoned the POA headquarters in Leeds. The man who answered told me that some kind of emergency meeting had been called in all of the prisons for the POA officers to attend, and that's probably why no one was answering my calls. However, he did say that there should still be someone to answer calls. He advised me to continue phoning, saying that someone should eventually pick up. Time wasn't on my side. Midday was quickly approaching. Bruce said to me that we would have to contact my solicitor and get his advice about what I should do. I phoned my solicitor. His secretary told me that he was in court all day and wouldn't be back in his office until after 4 p.m. Great! It was about ten minutes to midday. I tried the POA again. Someone answered. I explained to him what had happened and said that I had been trying to get in touch. He told me about the emergency meeting that had been called. He then told me that he hadn't really anything to do with the POA, but he would go get some advice for me and then call me back. I told him that I had to contact the prison before midday or else I would be put down as AWOL. I asked him if he would get back to me as soon as he could. He did get back to me within about ten minutes and informed me that he had spoken to a POA member who advised me to go on sickness leave until the matter could be sorted out. So I contacted Darren and told him what the POA had advised. I said that I was going on sickness leave. I had to get a self-certificate.

I made an appointment with my doctor. He put me straight on sickness leave, saying that I was experiencing stress. He then gave me a prescription for antidepressants. I didn't want this medication. He had checked my hair and had found that I was again suffering from alopecia, which was the result of the build-up from reoccurring incidents at the prison. I told my doctor that I didn't want to return to the prison, that I couldn't take any more of the grief that some of my co-workers kept throwing at me, and that I would always be looking over my shoulder and waiting for the next thing to happen if I returned to work. He advised me to take the medication, saying that in a little while I may feel differently about my future with the Prison Service.

The following day, I received a call from one of the main blokes in the POA. He asked me why I had gone on sickness leave. I explained everything to him and also explained that I had been to see my own doctor. I mentioned what my doctor had said, and then I told the POA representative that it was the POA that advised me to go on sickness leave until this matter was sorted out. He said that the POA should not have advised that. Whoever it was who told me to do that was wrong. I gave him the name of the person who had advised me. He said, "You shouldn't listen to him. He knows nothing." I told him that I would be sending in my sickness certificate. He said he would contact me within the next couple of days. I didn't know where I was. Even if I had intended to go back to the prison, I didn't know who was my manager or where I would be put within the prison. Even the POA didn't have a clue. I couldn't possibly go back under those circumstances.

My solicitor returned my call from the previous day and asked what had been going on and if I had gotten any joy with the POA. I told him that I didn't have a clue what was happening, saying that I had been wrongly advised by the POA and that I didn't want to return to the prison. My solicitor then asked me to come and see him the following day, at which time he would advise me properly and put me in the right direction. I felt that I had not much choice, really, so I arranged an appointment with him.

Bruce and I spoke at length that day regarding my future in the Prison Service. I admitted that I was devastated over the whole situation and that I had tried very hard, doing my job correctly, helping others whenever I could, and always being punctual and reliable, and yet I had been treated very badly. I deeply believed that I had been set up. Bruce also believed that I had been set up. He was gutted that it had come to this. He knew that I had loved my job and that I wanted to progress eventually in the Prison Service. He knew how much I had tolerated and what I had been through – and still I tried to battle on even though I had been tipped off that some people at work were trying to get me out. I couldn't really think straight. I felt deflated and useless. I felt like they had won and that I had lost. I thought that no matter what I did or how hard I tried, I was never meant to remain at that job. Bruce said that he would stand by me no matter what. If I decided to go back to the prison, then he would stand by me. If I decided to resign, then he would stand by me. He just wanted me to be happy. We both said that we would go see the solicitor on the following day and see what advice he gave us.

Grievance, Mediation, and Capability

On the following day, both Bruce and I attended the appointment with my solicitor. We told him everything that had happened. I brought him up to date regarding my having been wrongly advised by the POA and regarding where I stood with my doctor, my medication, etc. My solicitor was astounded by it all, astounded at my treatment from the prison and astounded at the POA. After he listened to all we had say, taking notes for more than two hours, he asked me what I wanted to do. I explained that I couldn't carry on the way I was at the prison, that I would always be looking over my shoulder and awaiting something else to happen. On the other hand, I said, it had been my dream job and I had always wanted to further my career in the Prison Service. But how could that possibly happen now? He advised me on many options: I could resign immediately; I could go down the path of the grievance procedure; and I could even request to transfer to another prison. Transferring to another prison seemed to be a good option at the time. I didn't want to return to the prison where I worked, as I knew that some people there had it in for me, I knew I would always be doomed. However, to transfer I would have to go with the grievance procedure. I opted for this. My solicitor said that he would first draft up a letter to be sent in to Dick. This letter, which would be drafted by the solicitor but sent from me, would clarify my position. My solicitor also suggest that the letter to be sent via the POA so that someone there could proofread it before Dick received it.

So the letter was drafted up. It basically confirmed the avoidance of doubt and stated that I was completely innocent of any alleged misconduct and would fully cooperate with any investigation that may be required. It also stated that my having to report for gate duties would have brought me into contact with work colleagues who had been involved with previous issues. The letter also stated that I had not received any official, written notification that I was under investigation or any formal notice that I was unable to continue with my present duties; therefore, the letter asked Dick for confirmation of my position at the present time. The letter then asked if the matter could be cleared up at the earliest opportunity. It was said in the letter that I was seeking to resolve the matter on an informal basis at that stage and that I didn't wish to resort to using the Prison Service's grievance procedure, but I reserved my right to do so in the event that matters weren't resolved at the earliest opportunity.

My husband hand-delivered this letter to the prison on the following day. It was clearly addressed to the POA. So I was expecting that maybe the following day or the day after I would get a call from Dick or receive some kind of acknowledgement of the letter. I received nothing. I waited around four days for some kind of reply, but none came. I contacted the POA to find out if someone there had proofread the letter and then handed it on to Dick. They had forgotten to do this. The letter was found in a drawer in the POA's office. It had not even been opened. So someone at POA proofread it, said it was fine, and forwarded it on to Dick. In the meantime, I had received an appointment to attend a meeting with the occupational health team. I had also received forms to fill in for my ill-health retirement. My solicitor advised not to fill in these forms, as it was probably the prison's way of trying to get rid of me.

A day or two later, I received a call from Dick saying that the deputy governor had offered me a place in the healthcare department until the investigation was conducted. Again, this was part of the gate area. If I took this post, then I would have the same manager and the same governor as the ones I had in reception. Also, the healthcare unit used the staff from reception to cover shifts on a daily basis, so basically I would have been working again with Lester, Darren, and Stef. I told Dick my position, saying that I had an upcoming appointment with Occupational Health and that Darren was going to meet with me after the appointment.

When I attended the Occupational Health appointment, which was held off the prison grounds, the woman who saw me advised me not to go back into the prison until the investigation had been conducted. She had seen my own doctor's report, saw how stressed I was about the whole situation, and knew I didn't have a mutually agreed position to return to. Darren was meant to come outside the prison grounds straight after my Occupational Health appointment, but as usual, he had gotten himself confused and had waited for me inside the prison, so I never got to see him that day.

I then began to feel an increasing amount of stress. I was advised not to go into the prison until the investigation had been conducted and until I knew my exact position, yet Dick and Darren informed me that the investigation could not be conducted until I returned to the prison. Having gotten myself into a state, I didn't know what to do, so I contacted the POA. Once again, no one was there to take my call, so I contacted the Leeds POA and spoke with a woman who said that she would immediately contact my local prison and have someone contact me within the day. That afternoon, I got a call from one of the POA members at the prison. My husband took the call, but he put the phone on loudspeaker so I could hear what was being said. My daughter was also there that day. My husband explained my situation, mentioning that I was stressed and was not very well. He said that I was advised not to go into the prison and yet the prison wouldn't conduct the investigation until I did. The POA rep said, "Look, mate, I am an officer and not a manager. My hands are tied. I can't do anything to help Liz. We are dealing with knobheads." So that was the advice from the POA, to which I had paid my subs each month. I contacted my solicitor, who said I had no option but to submit a grievance.

This I did. Again, my solicitor drafted the grievance submission for me, but it was sent to the prison as coming from me. I was allowed to take either a work colleague or a POA rep with me to the grievance hearing. The POA had previously made it clear that they wouldn't help me with this, so I opted to take Drew with me. I didn't really want to involve Mitch, as he was my best friend and I didn't want him to be put in any compromising situations. Drew was fully aware of my position. Plus, he had been present for the key incident.

The grievance hearing was held outside of the prison grounds. It was conducted by a governor who was often the acting deputy governor, so he was very high up in the prison hierarchy. My grievance submission included a chronology of the events leading up to my then-present position; a mention of what I considered to be my legitimate grievance; and a mention of what I considered to be an appropriate outcome, which was that my employer accept the chronology of events and my grievance issues as a fair representation of my position and that my employer acknowledge my position. Also, I requested that there be a clear discussion of and an agreement about where I would return and on what basis. In addition to that, I requested a clear understanding of and an agreement on which steps, if any, would be taken in relation to the key incident which had caused the difficulty. And finally I asked my employer to acknowledge that the situation, having regard to the sequence of events, could have been handled much better and more professionally, avoiding my unnecessary absence from work, the difficulties that had arisen, and the detriment to my health during that period.

All of this was put before the governor, who basically ripped me to bits. He said that he wouldn't put the fact that I was under investigation in writing as the investigation was now a "factfinder". He said that Darren had denied telling me to report for gate duties (even though Mitch had been present at the time and had witnessed this). He thought the situation could have been resolved if I had met with Darren following the Occupational Health appointment. He asked me to define the word *shock* since I had stated that I had gone into shock when Darren informed me of my suspension from the works department and of the investigation, as he claimed that shock would entail fainting or passing out. He said he couldn't comment on the lack of help from the POA, as that would be a separate grievance. He pulled me up on almost all of the grievance. His proposed outcome was either that I take the placement in healthcare until the factfinder had been conducted or that I consent to mediation between me, Darren, and Dick.

I passed this information to my solicitor, who informed me that it was time for him to get involved directly with the prison and make it known to them that he had been working on my behalf since the time of the incident that had occurred in 2011. He sent a letter to the prison direct from his company stating that he had been acting on my behalf and had done so in relation to my employment issues since January 2011. He stated that there were a number of things about the grievance outcome with which I didn't agree. He stated that these matters should be clarified either during the proposed mediation process or, if that was unsuccessful, during the appeal process. He also made it clear that I would be willing to go through the mediation process if an independent mediator was appointed and if the mediation took place off-site, at a neutral venue other than the prison. He gave the prison seven days to reply. Ten days later, there was still no reply, so he sent another letter, this one giving them another five days to reply; explaining that I was extremely anxious; and mentioning that my not hearing from them was adding to my level of stress. The prison did reply on the fifth day. They had arranged a mediation date, time, and place. This mediation session was cancelled twice by the prison, much to my despair. It eventually took place at the end of April 2012.

The mediation took place in Leeds and was scheduled for two days. The first day would be mediation between me and Darren, and the second day would be mediation between me and Dick. There were two mediators present. Unbelievably, they were from NOMS (National Offender Management Service), so they were definitely not independent. My mediation submissions were very similar to my grievance submissions, but they also included the bullying and harassment I was subjected to, my numerous questions about the day of the key incident, and Dick's inconsistent treatment of me. My required outcome was an acknowledgement that the grievances I had made in relation to being bullied and harassed had never fully been resolved; a clear agreement as to where I would return to work; a clear understanding of and an agreement as to what steps (if any) were to be taken in relation to the key incident; an acknowledgement that Darren's behaviour on 11 January had been unprofessional and had caused me to go into serious shock; an acknowledgement that I had been treated differently from my colleagues and an explanation as to why this was so; and, finally, an acknowledgement that Dick had behaved inappropriately and unprofessionally towards me and an explanation as to why he had done this.

The first day went extremely well with Darren. To be honest, I had presumed it would. He apologised for his unprofessional behaviour on 11 January, said he would do anything within his power to get me back to working alongside him again, and continued to apologise to me. The mediators felt the need to tell him in the end that he needn't apologise anymore. They agreed that mediation between Darren and me had gone well and that all had been resolved.

The following day with Dick was a different story, however. To begin with, he was late. The meeting was scheduled for 9 a.m., but he didn't turn up until 10.15. When we eventually got in the mediation room, I read out my statement, firstly asking what the outcome was for the incident with the key. Dick said that there were now going to be three procedures in place: the existing procedure for the keys; Dick's sitting down with me and discussing guidelines for security measures to be put in place; and Darren's being retrained so that he would speak better to his staff. I stated to Dick that I felt that I had been set up in this matter. Dick said he could not comment. After almost every matter that I put to Dick, he said he could not comment. I reiterated that I felt I had been set up, saying that I felt I could not return to the prison. At this point, the mediator said that it was not appropriate to carry on with mediation, but if both parties wished to do so, then we could keep mediation open, whether I returned to work or not. Dick agreed that mediation be kept on the table.

I contacted my solicitor as soon as I arrived home, but he was out of his office, so I passed on to his secretary what had occurred and how mediation had been left.

The following day, I received two letters from the prison. One asked how mediation had gone and then asked if I still wanted to pursue the grievance appeal. The other asked me to attend a capability meeting. I spoke with my solicitor, who advised me to attend the capability meeting and still pursue the grievance appeal. He wrote to the prison to confirm both of these appointments. The capability meeting was to be first, and the grievance appeal would be shortly after that. I decided to ask Mitch to attend the capability meeting with me, as I felt that when Drew had attended the grievance hearing with me, he didn't really back me up or give me the support that I deserved. Before I asked Mitch, he sent me a text message asking if I would like him to attend the meeting with me. Great minds think alike.

Again, the capability meeting was held outside the prison grounds. In attendance was a governor from security, a woman from human resources, me, and Mitch. When Mitch and I went into the meeting room, I noticed that the governor present was the same one who had carried on at me about the joiner working from the tool shed. "Great," I thought, "this is a fine start." He began by saying that it was his desire to resolve any issues that day. He asked what would help me to get back to work the following week. I replied by saying that I wanted to transfer to another prison. He said that that was not a realistic option, but he would not explain why. (I should note here that the issues I had had previously with regard to the bullying, my brothers, the key incident, and so forth would all be dealt with in the grievance appeal, so I was aware that these things wouldn't be discussed at this meeting.) The governor then asked me if there was anywhere in the prison where I would like to work, a place where I would feel comfortable. I told him that if it was not possible for me to get a transfer, then I would like to work in the inmates' library. I was aware that this was a job for an OSG. After I visited the library during my training and when I worked in reception, I wished to work in there. The woman from human resources butted in immediately and said that this was not an option, as there were no places open in the library, but the governor stopped her in her tracks and said that he could honour my request. If the library was where I would like to work, then the library it would be. I wasn't expecting him to say that I could work in the library. When he did, I was quite excited. All the bad thoughts I had been having about returning to the prison were beginning to fade away. The governor told me to go home, discuss it with my husband, have a good think about returning to the prison to work in the library, and contact him the following day to confirm. He also advised me to still pursue the grievance appeal, as I had issues that still required resolving.

When Mitch and I got outside, Mitch could see how pleased I was about working in the prison library. He was very happy that I was returning to the prison despite the fact that I wouldn't be working with him. I went home and discussed everything with Bruce. I also contacted my solicitor for advice. He advised me to return if I felt comfortable enough to do so. He said that he would prepare my grievance appeal submission, as that hearing was still to come. Bruce reiterated that he would stand by my decision no matter what.

I contacted the governor from security the following day and confirmed that I would return to the prison on the understanding that I would be working in the library. He said he would have everything in place by Monday morning. He told me that when I entered the prison, he would make sure Darren was there to meet me. The reason for this was that Darren would have to do the paperwork required for my return to work and then pass me over to a new manager.

Bullying of Inmates

On that Monday morning, I was very nervous, very apprehensive, and full of different expectations. I put on my uniform and headed to the prison. I was still unsure whether I was doing the right thing. It was still in the back of my mind what Molly had told me in regard to my being set up. All that I had gone through previously was rearing its ugly head in my mind, but I had to keep my thoughts positive. This was the job I had always wanted, to be in the Prison Service, and now I was given a chance to work in a department where I knew I could progress. It never bothered me, the thought of working so closely with the inmates. In fact, it could have only gone in my favour in future references, my having worked alongside Category A prisoners. So I put all the bad thoughts and apprehensions to the back of my mind and entered the prison. Darren was there, as planned, to meet me, which I was very glad about. I didn't fancy walking round the prison alone after everything that had happened. However, I got a real shock when I saw Darren, as he was in uniform. When he was my manager in the works department, he wore a suit and tie. So when I saw him in almost the same uniform as I was wearing, this indicated that he had been demoted. I remember how much he used to stress to me that he would hate it if ever he was put back in uniform. So the first thing I asked him was, "Why the uniform, Darren?"

It took him a while to answer me, but when he did, he said, "Long story, Liz, but I am no longer in the works. I am in the workshops, back working with the cons." I knew then that he had been demoted. I also knew that it was most probably the doings of Dick. I was gutted for Darren and hoped that it was not because of the key incident that this had happened.

Darren headed upstairs towards the security department. I asked him where we were going. He explained that he had found an office up there wherein he could do my return to work and fill in the appropriate paperwork. When we got in to the office, I asked him why we were not in the works department. He answered, "Dick said if I take you down there, he will kill you. He doesn't want you anywhere near him, and he is looking forward to the second mediation with you. Said he's gonna make your life a misery."

I looked at Darren and said, "Well, that's a nice welcome back." He just laughed.

We went through the return-to-work forms. When Darren got to the part asking which department we were working in, he began to write, "Security."

I stopped him and said, "Here. What ya doing? I am working in the library."

He looked at me as if I'd gone out of my mind. He said, "I was told you were working in security."

I started carrying on at Darren. I said, "I don't believe this. Governor assured me he would have it all in place by this morning for me to work in the library." Darren said we would go look for governor of security and find out what was going on.

This we did, but when we went into the security governor's office, we found a different governor sitting there. He explained that he was standing in, as the security governor was on leave. Immediately, I knew I had been blagged. I told the other governor exactly what had happened. He just looked confused. He said he was unaware of it all, which was typical. He asked Darren, "Why don't you take her down to the works department and see if there is anything she can do down there?"

Darren was just about to speak when I interrupted and said, "The works governor said if I go down there, he will kill me." Darren glared at me.

The governor just said, "Oh, I see. Better not send you there then." He said he would find an office for me to work in. He told me to do some filing until he could establish what was going on. Darren said he would try find Mr Angler, the one who took over after the incident with the mobile phones. Mr Angler was also the one who knocked me back for going to Willie's trial. He was also the one who investigated the key incident, and he was also the one who was demoted from principal officer to senior officer. The reason he got demoted was because he fought in the prison with another prison officer. Not only were two officers fighting within the establishment, but also they were fighting in the prison gym where all the inmates were working out. It was the inmates who had to break up the fight! Unbelievable. Can you imagine how that could have turned out if the inmates had not been sensible enough to stop the officers' fighting? It could have quite easily turned into a bloodbath. The brains that day in the gym were the inmates, not the staff. After that, Mr Angler faced disciplinary action and found himself demoted. I honestly do believe that one would have to commit murder to be sacked from that prison. Apparently, one can bully, intimidate, lose radios, change legal documents and put lives at risk, and fight with colleagues in front of inmates and still keep one's job – unless, of course, one, e.g. me or Keith, is disliked by Dick. In that case, one is doomed.

So the governor found a nice little office for me, pointed at the filing cabinets, told me what was in them, told me what to do, and showed me how to file documents. Darren had gone off looking for Mr Angler. I was left alone, but not for very long. Within a few minutes, Mitch came barging through the door. He had been up to the prison library thinking that I would be in there, but he couldn't find me. Then he saw Darren and asked him where I was. Mitch was as bemused as I and asked me why I was in the security department and not in the library. I told him what had been said that morning. I mentioned that the security governor was on leave. Immediately, Mitch said, "Liz, I sniff a rat."

"Me too," I said. "In fact, Mitch, it is a very large rodent that I am sniffing." We looked at each other and shook our heads. Mitch didn't stay very long before he was on his way. Darren came back into the office and said that he couldn't find Mr Angler. He believed that he was on leave that day too, so he told me just to continue with the filing. When my shift was over, he said, I should just leave the prison and then return the following morning to the same place. I couldn't believe that I was in the security department doing filing and that the governor who had promised me a place in the library was absent.

So I began with the duties that I had been given. Now that I have reached this part of my story, I will say that I believe that the stand-in governor that day will regret giving me those duties to do. What I was about to see was probably the worst thing I had witnessed throughout my entire time at the prison. I had witnessed a lot of wrongdoing, and I had endured bullying from other members of staff, but I was shocked to find out that reports of bullying from vulnerable inmates were swept beneath the carpet too. The documents I was filing were all of the SIRs (serious incident reports), only these SIRs had been submitted by inmates. Basically, when an inmate submits an SIR, it is sent to security for security to determine whether action should be taken and, if so, what action should be taken. If someone in security believes that no action is required, then he or she will ticked the appropriate box and then sign off on and file the SIR. So each SIR was ticked with either "action to be taken" (in which case it would be sent on for the matter to be dealt with) or "no action required" (in which case it would be filed).

I would say that around 80 per cent of the SIRs were ticked as "no action required", signed off on, and sent to be filed. And I would say that the majority of them were bullying-related. In reality, inmates had reported bullying, either after enduring bullying themselves or witnessing others being bullied, and their reports were filed under "no action required". Some of the submissions were horrible to read. I was appalled by what some inmates had endured and by the suffering caused to them by others, but their reports were simply filed and no action was taken. It was quite upsetting, especially when I knew that these reports were just being placed inside a filing cabinet. Then again, I had often thought previous to this time that if staff can be bullied by staff, then what chance did the inmates have?

I finished my shift, left the prison, and went home sluthened. I don't know if I was more upset because I wasn't yet in the library or because of the filing I had been doing. Either way, it had not been a good day. I filled Bruce in on my day. He couldn't believe the incompetence of the prison. I never mentioned anything about the filing I was doing, but I did tell him that I was in security and not yet in the library. He was astounded at the fact that the governor from the capability meeting had said that everything would be put in place but was on his annual leave when I returned. I mean, the governor must have been aware on the Thursday previous that he would be on annual leave on the following Monday. Had I just been blagged? I thought I had just been blagged. Plus, because I confirmed my return over the telephone with the governor, I had nothing about my place in the library in writing. But I thought I could be wrong. I figured that when I went back on the following day, the matter would be all sorted and I would be heading up to the library. So that night I tried not to think about it.

The following day, I went back into the prison. Lo and behold, I couldn't find anyone in the security department who could tell me anything about what was expected of me. I saw the governor from the day before and asked him what I should do. He took me back to the office where I had been filing. That particular door and filing cabinet were always kept locked. He was the only keyholder. It is no wonder to me that all of those filed documents were kept under lock and key, as the prison wouldn't want just anyone having access, not to the dust that was swept beneath the carpets.

Before he left the office, the governor told me to go make him a coffee in the kitchen that was situated just across from where I was working. On entering the kitchen, I noticed there was only one staff member in there. She had her back to me. I said hello as I walked across to the kitchen area. When she turned round, I saw that it was Eve's best friend! She looked at me like I was a turd on the pavement. I had to ask her which cup the governor used. She just pointed at it without saying a word. I made the drink as quickly as I could and was out of there. I took the coffee back to the governor and asked him how long it would be before I could go to the library. He basically told me the same thing as he had on the previous day, that he knew nothing about it. He said that I should just continue with the filing. I was well annoyed. I asked him to let me know if he saw Mr Angler or else if he would let Mr Angler know where I was. He said he would. I continued with the filing and hated every minute of it. Not very long into the morning, Darren came in to see me. He asked if I had seen anyone who could authorise my going to the library. I told him I would hopefully see Mr Angler, saying that I hoped that he could process my move. I asked Darren if he could possibly get hold of the final outcome from the reception case, as I would require it for the grievance appeal. I also asked for the outcome of the Adam and Eve case. He said he would do his best. He later returned and said that he was still awaiting an email about the reception case. In regard to the Adam and Eve case, he said he thought it would be a good idea if he arranged mediation within the prison for me, Mitch, Adam, and Eve. He said that he would be the mediator. I just laughed and said, "Darren, that's not going to happen, is it?"

He replied, "Funnily enough, I have just suggested the same to Mitch and he said exactly the same as you." I think Darren thought that because mediation had gone well between the two of us that it would go well with all us lot, but I still don't know how he thought he could be the mediator.

I continued with the filing after Darren had left. The more SRIs I read and had to file as "no action required", the more I got wound up. I felt like I was doing wrong by filing the SRIs while knowing that nothing was being done about the inmates' complaints. I felt like I was as bad as those who had made the bad decisions, as if I was agreeing to wrongdoing. It was an awful feeling.

A bit later, the office door opened and in walked Mr Angler. I was very glad to see him. All I could think about was the library. He asked me how I was and if I was enjoying working in security. I answered him with a question: did he have the authority to send me to the library? He said he was aware that I was going to the library and said it would be a really good job for me but he advised me to consider the different shift pattern I would be on. This was because some of the shifts in the library began at an extremely early time. One of the jobs in the library was dealing with the newspapers. This entailed reading through the daily newspaper to see if anything had been published about any inmate within the prison. If there was a story about an inmate, then the piece had to be cut out of each newspaper before any inmate could purchase one. Then there could be late shifts where audits were done and so forth. But as I told Mr Angler, different shifts and split shifts did not bother me in the least. So he said he would find out when my start date would be. I was annoyed at this because the governor from the capability meeting was supposed to have put all this in place for when I returned on the Monday. I stressed this to Mr Angler. He said to leave the matter with him, telling me that he would get back to me. He asked me if I had any other concerns, so I told him my concerns about the filing I was doing. I asked him why the inmates' accusations of bullying were just being filed and why no action was taken. His answer was, "Why? Do you really care about those nonces? Do you know how long it would take to process all that lot?" He more or less confirmed my suspicion that bullying is swept beneath the carpet because dealing with it entails too much paperwork and also because some of the reporters may be incarcerated for sex offences, which makes it OK to ignore their complaints. I tried to say that we prison workers had a duty of care towards the inmates, but the governor cut me off and said, "Don't worry about it, Liz. You are too nice."

I replied, "It's nice to be nice." After he left the office, I continued with the filing.

I then came across some quite disturbing SIRs. One indicated that an inmate had stopped going to the serveries for his meals because he was bullied by one of the servers. It had started because, I believe, the inmate had run up a debt with the server, so the server was removing food from the inmate's plate as a way of getting his debt paid back. But the situation got out of hand. The server began taking all of the inmate's food from his plate. When there was nothing left, he would give him a smack. So it reached the stage where the inmate stayed in his cell at mealtimes and didn't eat at all. The inmate put in an SIR, which was ticked "no action required". I then wondered if security staff ticked that box because they had the matter sorted or else saw that it had been resolved. But then I thought that this couldn't be the case, because the SIR would still have to be processed as a report. So why on earth would prison staff ignore the fact that an inmate was actually starving? If an inmate goes on a hunger strike, then that inmate is put on a feeding drip in order to keep him or her alive. I don't know what happened to this particular inmate or what his family must have thought when they visited and saw how much weight he had lost.

Then I came across another disturbing SIR that I had to file. This report had actually been put in by an inmate who was witnessing another inmate being bullied. He had put in the report because he was concerned for the other inmate, given with the latter's state of mind. According to the report, the inmate was very vulnerable and had gotten himself into debt. The bullying began once he did not repay the debt. He began to be physically harmed by other inmates, who must have started mentally torturing him. He became a wreck. The inmate who had reported this made a statement saying that he believed the bullied inmate was becoming suicidal. This SIR was ticked as "no action required" and was signed. What I found more disturbing was that, as I was going through more SIRs, I found another one, this one from the bullied inmate himself. The report was dated around two weeks after the first "no action required" one. The inmate had reported that he had received a threat from an inmate on the wing to which he was about to return. It turns out that he was returning to the wing after being in the healthcare unit. He had tried to take his own life. This SIR had actually been ticked as "action to be taken". However, it is my belief that if the first SIR had been dealt with correctly, then the inmate would not have tried to take his own life.

There were many, many reports that were similar to the one just mentioned. Another one was aimed at an officer who was purposely refusing to let an inmate go back to his cell during association. The inmate was afraid of a number of inmates who had been bullying him and, therefore, had asked to be locked in his cell during association, as he felt safer there. But a particular officer refused his request and made him go to association, where he was clearly being bullied. This SIR was also marked "no action required".

I am fully aware that a lot of the men who are incarcerated at this prison have committed horrendous crimes and that many people, especially the victims' families and other loved ones, would wish more than bullying upon them. I cannot begin to imagine what many people must have gone through in relation to what some of these inmates have done to end up in prison. However, being a staff member within the Prison Service means adhering to the prison rules and to the duty of care. I believe it takes a certain type of person to work in a prison and to work alongside inmates who have committed terrible, unforgivable crimes. Each person who applies for the role of prison worker is fully aware of where he or she will be working and of the type of people whom he or she will be working with and looking after. It is my belief that if you are a bullying, corrupt, underhanded, malicious, devious, and totally heartless person, then you have a good chance of making a career in the Prison Service. If you are a decent, honest, loyal, and conscientious person, then you have no chance of making it.

I felt like taking all of the SIRs to the security governor, plonking them on his desk, and asking what he was going to do about them. But what was the point? Hardly anyone in that prison did anything by the book. Most everything was covered up. Managers stuck together, and lower-ranking workers had no chance. SIRs were simply put away and not dealt with. I bet that the SIR Mitch and I put in regarding Dick and the road pin was ticked as "no action required" and then signed. The whole reporting process was a joke. Still, I was feeling guilty for having to file the SIRs when I was aware of what was going on.

I finished my shift. Mr Angler had not come back to see me and Darren had not come back, so I left the prison and went home.

My third day of being in security had arrived. It was just the same as it was on the two previous days. I worked in a tiny little office with no windows, no colleagues, and no information. I would have been better in a cell on the wings. In that event, at least I would have had someone to talk to. After I endured about four hours of what felt like solitary confinement, Mr Angler came barging into the office. All smiles, he was holding two cups of coffee. "Now then, Liz, I have some news."

"Yes," I thought, "bring on the library." He sat down, handed me a coffee, and told me that there was no place available for me in the prison library. I would go on the waiting list, but it might be around three or four months before a place came up. Then he told me that they were short-staffed in security. Since I was doing such a good job in clearing the backlog of files, I would remain where I was, he told me. I was furious, I knew I had been blagged. I tried arguing it out with him, but he wasn't interested. He told me that I shouldn't have been promised a place in the library – and that was it. He swiftly left the office and left me distraught. It was approaching lunchtime. I really needed to get out, so I began packing up the files. I was just ready to leave when Darren came into the office. I told him what Mr Angler had said. He looked at me very dubiously but made no comment. There was something else on his mind; I could sense it. "What is it, Darren?" I asked.

"You are not going to be happy," he said. Then he told me that he had been trying to get the documentation for me from the reception case. After having no joy, he had gone to see Darren personally (the other Darren who had investigated the reception case). Darren from reception had said that there was no paperwork, as the outcome was "no findings".

"What the hell does that mean?" I asked Darren. He said that when he spoke to the other Darren, the latter had said that the reception staff had denied the accusations. To save on an otherwise vast amount of paperwork, the matter had been closed as "no findings".

"What? He told you that?" I asked. Darren just nodded his head. He then said how wrong it all was, mentioning that I had obviously been lied to when I was told that the case had been left open and that the reception staff had been given warnings. And like Darren said, I had gotten nothing in writing regarding the outcome. Because then I was still quite new to the Prison Service, I had not been aware of the correct procedures, so I had just trusted that what Darren from reception had said was correct.

Darren told me to go on my lunch break and to try to calm down. When he left the office, I just sat with my head in my hands, not believing what I had just been told. I began thinking of all the things the staff had done to me in reception: hating the fact I was a woman, hardly conversing with me (and when they did it was to have a pop at me), locking me in the prop room, giving me food off the floor, and stitching me up. I could have gone on and on thinking of the bad things they did to me and how they had made me ill. Then on top of this, what with Mr Angler telling me I had no place in the library, that I was going to be stuck in that pokey office in security filing corrupt documents, I realised that basically I had been had. Well, that was it. I had taken enough. I got my bag and coat and went through the search area. As I dropped my prison keys down the key chute, I knew that this time would be the last time. I walked out of the prison and never looked back. I knew 100 per cent this time that I would never return.

Grievance Appeal and Resignation

My solicitor saw me more or less straightaway after I had walked out of the prison. He admitted that he had made a mistake by advising me to return to work without first having something in writing with regard to my alleged job in the library. He said in hindsight that we should have waited for the library job to be put in place and a phase return schedule put in place – and that we should have gotten everything in writing prior to my return. Regarding the reception case, he told me not to worry too much about it, as I had the interview regarding the investigation in writing, which proved that the allegations had been made, but nothing in writing regarding how the investigation had been dealt with. He advised me to attend the grievance appeal. He knew as well as I did that the appeal would probably not resolve anything, but he was intrigued to learn how the prison would deal with that and with the fact that I had been promised a job in the library when there was a witness, Mitch, present.

Within a day or two, I received a letter from Governor Number One stating that I had returned to work but after three days had failed to attend, so she invited me to another capability meeting in her office the following week. My solicitor responded to her immediately, requesting that the meeting be postponed until I had attended the grievance appeal and received the outcome. Governor was happy to accommodate our request.

Three days prior to the grievance appeal, my solicitor had sent into the prison my submissions for the appeal. In case of any doubt, and knowing how incompetent the prison was, he sent one copy to Governor Number One, one copy to the head of the panel for the grievance appeal, and one copy to human resources. I also had a copy to take with me. In the submissions, my solicitor had asked the panel to consider the fact that if a POA member were to be present, then this would be a conflict of interest.

Once again, Mitch was in attendance with me. My solicitor strongly advised this, as Mitch had been a witness at the capability meeting when I was promised the library job. This meeting was held outside of the prison grounds. On arrival, Mitch and I were greeted by the head man from the POA! He asked how I was and told me I had nothing to worry about. Then he explained that the reason he was present was that at the time of the key incident I was in the POA and could still be represented. At this early stage, I suspected that the appeal panel had not seen the grievance submission. The POA guy took Mitch and me into a meeting room and asked me if I wanted him to sit in for the meeting. I told him I didn't want him to sit in and said that I would be fine with Mitch. He said he would hang around in the building in case I needed anything.

The panel members entered the room. There were three of them: the main man, who apparently was the head of reoffending; a woman, whom I believe was from human resources; and a POA member (the same one who had said to my husband that we were dealing with knobheads). The main man opened up the meeting and asked me what I was expecting from the grievance appeal. Before we went any further, I asked if he had read through the grievance submission. He said he had not seen it, had not been given it, and didn't have a copy of it. I gave him my copy. He then said we should stop the meeting while the three of them went to make a copy of my copy and also read through it. Approximately thirty minutes passed before they returned. The first thing the main man commented on was the POA. He asked if I wanted the POA member to leave and have just the two panel members. I said yes. The POA member then left.

The man leading the meeting then spoke about mediation. For some reason, he had been told that I had mediated only with Darren. I put him right and told him that I had mediated with both Darren and Dick, and that mediation was successful with Darren but not with Dick. He then seemed to focus a lot on the report of the capability meeting that had been held with the security governor. He asked both Mitch and me what I had been offered in regards to returning to work. We both informed him exactly what I had been offered and exactly what had been said. He had the minutes in front of him from the capability meeting and could clearly see that the offer of the library spot had been omitted from the minutes. He said that my phased return should have been done before I returned to work and should have stated clearly my hours of work and the place of my work. He then asked me if I had the key investigation's outcome in writing. I said no. I also told him that neither did I ever receive an outcome in writing regarding the investigation conducted in reception. He was writing all this down while I was speaking. He then said that he had gotten a magic wand. He asked how I would feel if he waved the magic wand and got me a job in the prison library. I asked if I could have that in writing. He never answered me. So I asked him about a possible transfer to another prison. He said he was unsure about this, as he did not deal with transfers. The woman from HR said that the prison didn't often transfer OSGs, only in extreme circumstances, but she told me that she would look into it. She and the man continued sifting through my submissions. The main man said he would look into the issues raised and write to me with an outcome within ten days.

I received the outcome within a week. There was nothing constructive at all in it. There was no mention of the issues raised. The letter basically advised me to go ahead with the mediation with Dick. There was nothing in writing as to where I would be placed if I returned to the prison. It was very similar to the outcome I received after my original grievance hearing. I took the report to my solicitor. He said that if I was adamant about not returning to submit my resignation, he believed that I now had enough evidence to take the prison to a tribunal so that I could receive a constructive dismissal. Before he prepared my resignation, my solicitor sought advice from a barrister. To be able to sue for constructive dismissal, one needs a 51 per cent chance or higher of winning. The barrister assessed my case as well over 51 per cent. So my solicitor prepared my resignation, stating that I had been let down on so many occasions by my employer that it was difficult to say how the requirement of trust and confidence could be restored. After all, it had been substantially breached. The letter of resignation was sent in to Governor Number One and was also hand-delivered to the prison.

Within a few days, I received a letter from Governor Number One saying that she had received my resignation. She stated in the letter that I had clearly made my decision because of a number of factors. She mentioned that it was always a source of regret when a member of staff wished to leave the organisation. She stated that she understood that one of the factors affecting my decision was the recent correspondence I had received explaining the outcome of my grievance. She was concerned about my decision and believed it would be good practice to allow me a period of five days to review my decision and to be clear in my mind that this was the course of action I wished to take.

My mind was made up. I had no intention of reconsidering. My solicitor prepared another letter asking Governor Number One to look at all the accompanying correspondence, which was a full chronology of events, and also asking if she would like to discuss these issues either formally or informally. Governor wrote back accepting my resignation with a four-week notice. She stated that arrangements would be made for my uniform and prison-issue belongings to be collected.

I was quietly gutted, gutted because all I had ever tried to do was my job to the best of my ability. I had never done any wrong in that prison, yet many people there made my life a misery and a living nightmare. They had done many bad things to me and had let me down on many occasions, but I was the one who had to walk away. I do not wish to blow my own trumpet, but I know I would have made a good prison officer given the chance. I would have been fair and would definitely not have consented to any form of bullying. But, as I wrote earlier, it seems that the bad ones clearly get on and the good ones suffer.

My friend Mitch was extremely upset that things had come to this point. He said to me that he had lost the best colleague he had ever worked with. I could have said the same, as he was the best colleague and friend I had ever had. When Darren came to my home to collect my uniform and prison-issue belongings, he was truly gutted too. He gave me a huge hug and told me that if I ever needed references or anything like that, he would give the best for me.

Injustice

My next appointment with the solicitor was to discuss the tribunal for my constructive dismissal. He mentioned the witness statements we would require from my former colleagues and suggested that it would be a massive help if we could get a statement from Molly or from her brother who had been told that the prison was trying to set me up. The solicitor told me and Bruce how much it would cost to get the case to a tribunal. He also told us that we had three months minus a day from the date of my resignation to submit the ET1 (forms for the tribunal).

Not many people will believe me when I say that I wasn't taking the prison to a tribunal because I wanted money. I wanted justice. I wanted the prison to take the blame and be answerable for what some of its staff had done. I didn't want any other person to suffer in the way I had, and I wanted the bullying inside of the prison, whether it be the bullying of staff or of inmates, to end.

My solicitor told me that if I were to be successful, I would probably be looking at an award of around thirty-five grand. The most a tribunal would pay out was seventy-two grand. Well, thirty-five grand wasn't even two years' wages, so it wouldn't have been a life-changing amount of money. At that time, I would have been quite happy just getting enough money to cover the legal fees that Bruce and I had paid to the solicitor. At that time, it had cost us around five grand, but we still had to fund getting the case to a tribunal. As I said before though, the main thing I wanted was justice. I also wanted to be heard.

My solicitor explained that my resignation went in on 26 June 2012 with four weeks' notice, which took it to 26 July 2012. So with the three months minus a day in mind, the ET1 would have to be submitted before 25 October 2012. He told Bruce and me to try to take a holiday or a break and forget the matter for a few weeks. He was going away on holiday himself, so we knew we wouldn't be hearing from him for a few weeks.

In the weeks after my resignation, I was working on the witness statements. Mitch said he was quite happy to do one. I never doubted that he would. Mitch had asked Drew if he would do a witness statement, as Drew was present during the key incident and was also present at the first grievance hearing. Drew didn't want to get involved. I can totally understand why staff wouldn't want to get involved, as I had been there myself. I am fully aware of the consequences when one goes against a fellow officer or, even worse, a manager or a governor. However, I did find out later that I had been back-stabbed by Drew. Prior to the Adam and Eve case, Drew had told both Mitch and me that he would be a witness in the investigation, as he despised Adam and Eve. Plus, Adam had previously bullied Drew, so Drew felt it was the right thing to do. He even told Dick he would be a witness. Then apparently, not long after he had attended the grievance hearing with me, he wrote a letter to Governor Number One stating that he wished to withdraw his witness statement for the Adam and Eve case. I am still unsure if he did this because he didn't want to be involved or because he had been influenced by people of higher grades either before or after the grievance hearing.

I also approached Molly in regard to what her brother had told her about the prison trying to set me up. She didn't want to make a witness statement at that time as she was very close to taking early retirement. Also, just as I was, she was fully aware of the consequences she would face if she came forward. I understood this. Still, I think that it is beyond sad when staff fear coming forward and doing the right thing because they fear losing their jobs.

October was fast approaching. Bruce and I often contacted the solicitor to make sure that the ET1 was prepared and ready to be submitted to the court. Unbelievably, the solicitor left it right until the day before 25 October 2012. I don't know if this is some type of method that solicitors use, but it had me and Bruce panicking. Anyway, the ET1 was prepared. My solicitor emailed it to me and asked if I thought anything should be added to it. There were a few things I thought should be added, so I told my solicitor about them. He agreed with my points, but he said we could add them later when the witness statements were submitted. For the time being, the main thing was to get the ET1 application submitted.

So the ET1 was submitted. My solicitor received confirmation that it had been received. Within a few days, we received the dates for the tribunal, which was to take place in the following March. Before then, quite a bit of preparation would have to be done on the case. A barrister would have to be sought. Statements and so forth would have to be exchanged between m and the Prison Service.

At the beginning of December, I received an email from my solicitor. Before I opened the email, I presumed that he had sent it to ask for some more paperwork in regard to my case. I was wrong. There was an attachment to the email which my solicitor asked me to read. He also asked me to make an appointment to meet with him. The attachment was a letter from the home office stating that the ET1 submission would be dismissed, as my solicitor had submitted the ET1 out of time. At first, I presumed he had gotten the dates wrong and maybe had submitted the ET1 a day late or something like that. But the home office claimed that the period of three months minus a day started on the date of my letter of resignation and not on the first day of my four-week-notice period. So basically the home office was claiming that the last date to submit the ET1 was 25 September. They determined this by using the actual date of my resignation letter, which was 26 June, and not 25 October, which was the date my solicitor had presumed began the period of three months minus a day. In other words, the ET1 was one month late.

Both Bruce and I went to see the solicitor immediately. He said that his belief was that the people at the home office were clutching at straws, as they could see I had a very good case and were trying anything to get it thrown out of court. He said we would appeal against their decision. This we did. I had to attend the appeal court in Leeds in January of 2013. The solicitor sent a barrister to defend the appeal. The solicitor's firm funded this barrister. My solicitor didn't attend the appeal court. Bruce and I met with the barrister about an hour before the case so we could go through some paperwork. When we were called through to the court, we saw quite a few officials from the home office present, one being the woman who had attended my grievance appeal. So it was my barrister against the barrister from the home office. The two argued their points for quite some time as the judge made lots of notes. The appeal was finished in the late afternoon. My solicitor and I were informed that we would hear through letter the judge's decision within six weeks.

So now it was a case of playing the waiting game. There was nothing I could do until I received the judge's decision. Lo and behold, six weeks to the day I got an email from my solicitor. The judge's decision was attached to that email. I had won the appeal. Brilliant! The case was back on track. My solicitor was very relieved by this decision, for obvious reasons. So the judge had ruled that we were not out of time, that the date would be taken from the 26 July and not the 26 June. We received a new date for the tribunal. It was now going to take place in October 2013. Bruce, my solicitor, and I knew that this was a setback, but at the same time we were all very relieved that I had won the appeal and that my case was back on track.

In the following month, April, I received a letter from the home office. They were appealing against my appeal! I couldn't believe it. I was devastated. And this time it would be in the appeal court in London in front of a High Court judge. The date had been set for July 2013.

Then, as if things couldn't get any worse, my solicitor refused to send a barrister to London. He said that Bruce and I would have to pay seven grand if we wanted a barrister sent. It was my solicitor's mistake that had gotten me in this position – and he wasn't prepared to fight his own battle in court. He also stressed that I would need a barrister to defend the case, especially in the appeal court in London. It was as if he was saying that I needed a barrister but that his office wouldn't fund one, so the only option I had was to pay his office seven grand so that the workers there could defend themselves. Bruce and I couldn't afford to pay this amount of money. We had already paid my solicitor almost six grand by now. I was out of work, having lost a job that had paid me nineteen grand a year. There was no way we could raise this amount of money without remortgaging our home or going into debt. Plus, there was no guarantee that I would win the case. This would be the final appeal and the final decision. I took a few days to mull everything over, and then I made a huge decision: I would defend myself. I knew it was a brave decision, but I didn't want the prison to win without a fight. I contacted the home office and informed them that I would still go ahead with the appeal. I said that I would be representing myself and would have no legal representation.

Over the next few weeks, I sent a lot of paperwork to and received a lot of paperwork from the home office by using the Internet. I was out of my league and didn't have the first clue about what I was doing. Bruce and I began to research all the legalities of how to prepare for an appeal, what the case laws were, etc. Some nights, we were still up at 3 a.m. or 4 a.m., going through the prison case, case laws, and appeal procedures. This was all just to get the correct paperwork sent in preparation for the appeal. Then I had to prepare my own submission and read the one from the home office. I was losing to the will to live. My family and friends were all astonished that I had made the decision to defend myself at the London appeal court, but they admired me very much for not just throwing in the towel.

Both Bruce and I decided that we would travel down to London the day before the appeal, as we were due in court before 10 a.m. Bruce had to take two days off work. We booked a hotel and headed off on the day before the appeal. This was more cost we incurred, the travel, the hotel, the time off work. We even ended up getting three fines over those two days, for a congestion charge and a parking ticket, the latter because we were late getting back from the appeal court and our meter had expired. We weren't aware of the congestion charge, as we only ever went to London on organised tours to Wembley or to the theatre.

The morning of the appeal soon came round. I couldn't eat my breakfast in the hotel because I was too uptight and nervous. I was thinking all the time that this was my last chance. I had been informed that the decision would be made straightaway, that I wouldn't have to wait weeks for the outcome. Bruce and I got a cab at the hotel and went to the appeal court. We were a little early, so we went to get a coffee. While I was sitting and drinking my brew, my brother Willie rang me. He reassured me that I was doing the right thing, and he told me to be myself and to speak my mind. He reminded me that it was the same court he had been in when he had appealed against a prison sentence and had won his appeal. He wished me luck, told me he loved me, and said goodbye.

When Bruce and I got into the court, we had to sit right outside the courtroom that was booked for us. Also there was the barrister from the home office who had been at the first appeal in Leeds. He kept coming over to us to give us updates about how long it would be before the judge was ready to commence. He even shook my hand and wished me luck. At around 11 a.m., we were called in. There were quite a few people in the court. I didn't recognise any of them except for their barrister, of course. It was scary because I was sitting at the long desk where the barristers sit just below the judge. Bruce was allowed to sit by my side. Once the judge entered the courtroom, we all stood. He didn't look as old as I had expected. I don't know why but I expected him to be a really old judge, but I did. He looked to be maybe in his late fifties. He looked stern and unfriendly. I was a bit scared. But as the day progressed, I realised that looks are deceiving. The judge was a true gentleman. He was very soft-spoken and was kind and considerate. Throughout the morning, he kept looking at me and giving me reassuring looks and little smiles. So before I had even spoken, he had made me feel a little bit more at ease.

The hearing was very similar to the first appeal. The barrister from the home office was up for quite a lengthy time while raising his points and reading out case laws. He later finished, closed his files, and sat down. I knew it was my turn. My knees were weak and my mouth had gone dry. I was just about to stand up when the judge said, "Please don't stand. Remain seated." Then he explained to me directly that he was fully aware that I had no legal representation and that he thought I was very brave to come and defend not myself, but a mistake that my solicitor had made. He went on to say that I did not have to give any legal evidence, as it was the home office making the appeal and not me, so it was their barrister who had to argue against the first judge's ruling. The judge then explained that there was no actual case law even similar to this case and that my case would most probably make a new case law. He then asked me if there was anything I would like to say to him.

After I said, "Yes," I began to stand. The judge told me again to remain seated. I said that I felt it would be unfair if my case were not heard in a court of law. I mentioned that I was not a solicitor or barrister and that I had no legal expertise. I was just an ordinary woman who went to work and did my job correctly and got penalised for doing so. I voiced that I felt a tribunal was necessary in order to enable officials to put things right in the Prison Service, to stop the bullying that I had not only endured but also witnessed. I said that I didn't wish anyone else to suffer the way I had suffered and the way others suffered.

The judge wrote everything down that I said. When I had finished, he smiled at me and said, "Thank you very much. And thank you for coming here today and showing bravery and determination."

He then adjourned and told us to return to the court in two hours. He would have his decision by that time. I just took a deep breath. In a way, I was relieved that it was almost over. I knew that I didn't have to say anything else in court. It was done now. It all lay in the hands of the judge. No matter what the decision was going to be, there would be nothing more that anyone could do. The judge's decision would be the final decision.

Bruce and I went out and got a bite to eat. I think those two hours were the longest two hours I have ever endured. I was fidgeting and pacing up and down. I just couldn't stay still. My nerves were shot. It was a terrible feeling. I don't know how a person feels when he or she is on trial and the jury goes out to deliberate, especially if the person is innocent.

Bruce and I returned to the courtroom and awaited the judge. When he entered the courtroom, he gave me a lovely smile. He then began to speak to the court, explaining once again why we were all there and then going over the paperwork that had been submitted. He went quite in depth by mentioning cases similar to mine, but none were exactly the same as mine. Then finally he said, "The fact that governor in her letter stated that the respondent was required to give four weeks' notice and that, therefore, the respondent's last working day would be 27 July 2012 – and given that she was paid for that period – has, in my view, no legal effect. As a matter of law, the respondent resigned on 29 June 2012. She terminated the contract under which she was employed without notice by reason of the appellant's conduct. The effective date of termination was 29 June 2012. Accordingly, the unfair dismissal claim was lodged out of time and the employment tribunal has no jurisdiction to hear it. For the reasons I have given, the appeal succeeds."

I had lost – lost my right to be heard, lost my chance to try to make a difference and stop bullying, and lost complete faith in the legal system.

The judge then spoke directly to me and asked me for the name of my solicitor. He said, "I am so sorry that you have lost your right to be heard, but the law is the law. If I could do any different for you, I would. I can see you are a genuine lady. I have felt strongly in regard to your being heard and showing much bravery. I wish you all the very best for the future, my dear." I thanked the judge for his kind words. Everyone then left the courtroom.

Outside, the barrister for the home office approached Bruce and me and offered his condolences. He also said he was sorry for me. He told me that the person who had lost my right was my solicitor. He said that when one pays for legal representation, it should never come to this. I didn't say very much to him, as I didn't like him. I know he had a job to do and was only doing his job, but he was part of why I lost my right. I disliked him for that.

Bruce and I then had a long journey home from London. We were depleted, tired, and gutted, just wanting to get home.

To do my own summing up, I had been subjected to bullying, harassment, and victimisation during my time working at the prison. I had seen and witnessed the bullying of other staff and of inmates. My life had been made a misery at the hands of self-righteous, arrogant prison officers and managers. I had suffered from immense stress, sleepless nights, and alopecia. I had to have counselling to help me build my confidence and to help ease my bad thoughts about the staff and inmates who were still enduring bullying. I had lost my career and my pension. My family and I had suffered deeply. In return for all this, the prison staff brushed every incident beneath the carpet. They covered up bullying, harassment, and victimisation. The bullies all remain employed at that prison. The bullying of inmates will continue. The bullying of staff will continue.

My final words are these: if I can't get justice, then what chance has Charlie got?

Printed in Great Britain
by Amazon.co.uk, Ltd.,
Marston Gate.